He'd stayed away from Tori the past few weeks.

He'd had a tight feeling in his gut ever since his life had crossed with Tori's again. Ever since the night Andy had been born, he couldn't seem to disconnect himself from her and the baby she wanted to mother so badly.

Without a moment's hesitation, he slid closer to her and wrapped his arm around her. Even with his vast experience with words—the calm make-a-deal tone, the believe-and-you-can-trust-me phrases, the coaxing supplications, the firm stand-his-ground negotiation—in all of it there were no words for a situation like this. Tori was worried she'd lose her son in so many ways. He wouldn't give her platitudes that might not be honest.

When Tori's shoulders relaxed and she leaned against him, he knew she'd finally accepted his support. That seemed to be majorly important to him, and he didn't examine too closely the reasons why....

Dear Reader,

Well, the new year is upon us—and if you've resolved to read some wonderful books in 2004, you've come to the right place. We'll begin with *Expecting!* by Susan Mallery, the first in our five-book MERLYN COUNTY MIDWIVES miniseries, in which residents of a small Kentucky town find love—and scandal—amidst the backdrop of a midwifery clinic. In the opening book, a woman returning to her hometown, pregnant and alone, finds herself falling for her high school crush—now all grown up and married to his career! Or so he thinks....

Annette Broadrick concludes her SECRET SISTERS trilogy with *MacGowan Meets His Match.* When a woman comes to Scotland looking for a job *and* the key to unlock the mystery surrounding her family, she finds both—with the love of a lifetime thrown in!—in the Scottish lord who hires her. In *The Black Sheep Heir,* Crystal Green wraps up her KANE'S CROSSING miniseries with the story of the town outcast who finds in the big, brooding stranger hiding out in her cabin the soul mate she'd been searching for.

Karen Rose Smith offers the story of an about-to-be single mom and the handsome hometown hero who makes her wonder if she doesn't have room for just one more male in her life, in *Their Baby Bond.* THE RICHEST GALS IN TEXAS, a new miniseries by Arlene James, in which three blue-collar friends inherit a million dollars—each!—opens with *Beautician Gets Million-Dollar Tip!* A hairstylist inherits that wad just in time to bring her salon up to code, at the insistence of the infuriatingly handsome, if annoying, local fire marshal. And in Jen Safrey's *A Perfect Pair,* a woman who enlists her best (male) friend to help her find her Mr. Right suddenly realizes he's right there in front of her face—i.e., said friend! Now all she has to do is convince *him* of this....

So bundle up, and happy reading. And come back next month for six new wonderful stories, all from Silhouette Special Edition.

Sincerely,

Gail Chasan
Senior Editor

Their Baby Bond

KAREN ROSE SMITH

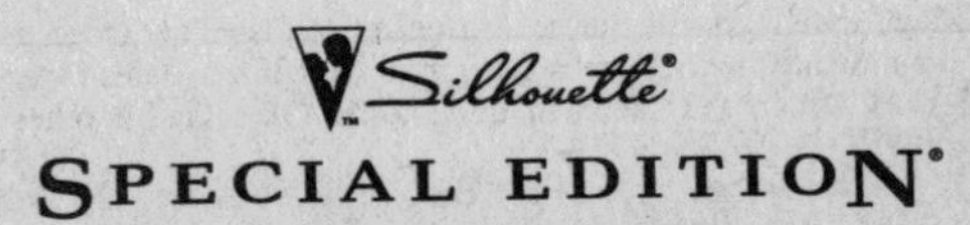

Published by Silhouette Books
America's Publisher of Contemporary Romance

In memory of my grandparents, Antonio and Rosalie Arcuri,
who gave me my first glimpse of life outside of Pennsylvania.

With thanks to Jill Brown, who patiently explained the answers to my questions about pyloric stenosis. In appreciation to Megan Walsh, an expert on adoption in New Mexico. With deepest thanks to Detective Jeff Arbogast, Public Informations Officer for the Albuquerque Police Department. Their expertise and experience were invaluable.

SILHOUETTE BOOKS

ISBN 0-373-24588-2

THEIR BABY BOND

This edition published by arrangement with Harlequin Books S.A.

Visit Silhouette at www.eHarlequin.com

Printed in U.S.A.

Books by Karen Rose Smith

Silhouette Special Edition

Abigail and Mistletoe #930
The Sheriff's Proposal #1074
His Little Girl's Laughter #1426
Expecting the CEO's Baby #1535
Their Baby Bond #1588

Silhouette Books

The Fortunes of Texas
Marry in Haste...

Silhouette Romance

**Adam's Vow* #1075
**Always Daddy* #1102
**Shane's Bride* #1128
†*Cowboy at the Wedding* #1171
†*Most Eligible Dad* #1174
†*A Groom and a Promise* #1181
The Dad Who Saved Christmas #1267
‡*Wealth, Power and a Proper Wife* #1320
‡ *Love, Honor and a Pregnant Bride* #1326
‡*Promises, Pumpkins and Prince Charming* #1332
The Night Before Baby #1348
‡*Wishes, Waltzes and a Storybook Wedding* #1407
Just the Man She Needed #1434
Just the Husband She Chose #1455
Her Honor-Bound Lawman #1480
Be My Bride? #1492
Tall, Dark & True #1506
Her Tycoon Boss #1523
Doctor in Demand #1536
A Husband in Her Eyes #1577
The Marriage Clause #1591
Searching for Her Prince #1612
With One Touch #1638
The Most Eligible Doctor #1692

*Darling Daddies
†The Best Men
‡ Do You Take This Stranger?

Previously published under the pseudonym Kari Sutherland

Silhouette Special Edition

Wish on the Moon #741

Silhouette Romance

Heartfire, Homefire #973

KAREN ROSE SMITH

Award-winning author Karen Rose Smith first glimpsed the Southwest on a cross-country train ride when she was sixteen. Although she has lived in Pennsylvania all her life, New Mexico has always called to her. The mountains there have a power and beauty she hopes she managed to convey in this book. Readers can reach Karen at her Web site (www.karenrosesmith.com) or write to her at P.O. Box 1545, Hanover, PA 17331.

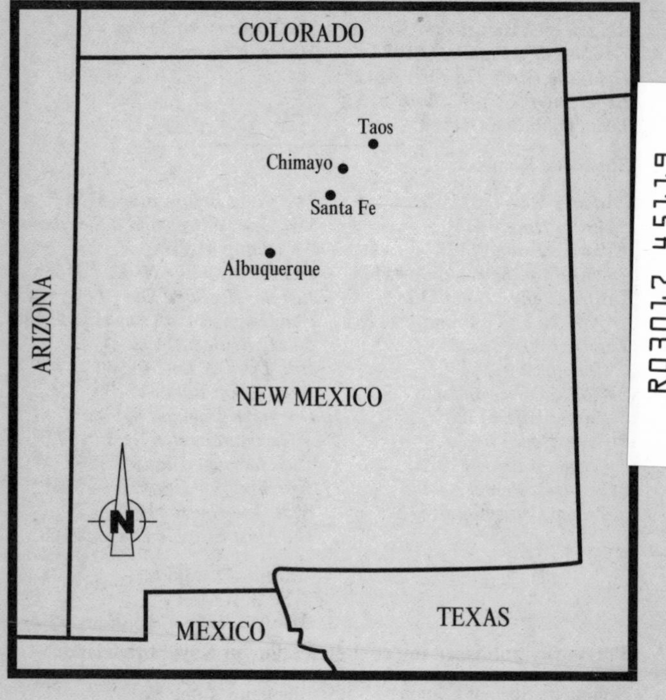
COLORADO
Taos
Chimayo
Santa Fe
Albuquerque
ARIZONA
NEW MEXICO
N
MEXICO
TEXAS

Chapter One

Excitement, anticipation and fear danced inside Victoria Phillips all at the same time. In less than a month, she'd be bringing home a baby.

Deep purple and muted orange streaked the early September Santa Fe sky as Tori hurried up the three steps to the porch of her adobe ranch-style house. She let herself inside, thinking again about bringing home her baby boy if all went as planned…if Barbara Simmons—the eighteen-year-old who wasn't ready for motherhood—didn't change her mind. Tori had agreed to an unusual request, and now it haunted her more each day.

As she set her leather purse on the counter, her doorbell rang.

Quickly she returned to her living room. Maybe it was Barbara. She stopped in every now and then to report on all that was happening in her pregnancy. From the moment Tori had seen the sonogram of that little baby boy…

Swinging the door wide open, her breath caught as she recognized the man standing there—Jake Galeno. She'd called the number in his ad just last night. When she'd left a message, she'd never expected him to get back to her this soon, and certainly not show up on her doorstep! It had been twelve years since she'd last seen him, twelve years since he'd taken her to her prom and at the end of the evening given her a heart-stopping kiss she'd never forgotten.

In spite of the fact that she was a very confident thirty now, she was flustered. ''Jake! I didn't know if you'd remember me. I never expected you to get back to me this quickly.''

The breeze tossed his blue-black hair. The mixture of Native American, Spanish and Anglo heritage evident in his high cheekbones, angular face and slightly crooked nose reminded her she'd once thought he was the most handsome, the most sexy, man in the world.

He still is, a little voice whispered.

''Of course I remember you. How could I ever forget a night in Camelot?'' he teased.

She'd never forget her senior prom and the legendary world that had embraced them for one wonderful night. Jake Galeno's rugged outward appeal had always been enhanced by a deep, calm, sensual voice that vibrated through her like the ancient notes of the Native American music she loved. Now her thoughts scattered like dust in the wind as his almost-black eyes held hers for interminably long seconds.

Finally he stepped into the silence. ‘‘You called me because you have work you need to have done on your house?’’

He was going to think she was an absolute idiot! Brushing a few strands of her tawny, pageboy-cut hair behind her ear, she swallowed. ‘‘Yes, I did. Please come in.’’

When Jake moved into her house, he seemed to take up all the space. He was six-foot-two, broad-shouldered and lean-hipped. Due to her friendship with his sister, Nina, he’d taken her to the prom out of kindness. Afterward they’d gone their separate ways. Back then, he’d just finished training at the police academy and had taken a job on the Albuquerque police force. She wondered why he’d returned to Santa Fe.

‘‘You told me your work hours when you left your message,’’ he reminded her. ‘‘I looked up your address in the phone book. It will be easier to give you an estimate for your repairs if I see them.’’

‘‘The last two contractors I phoned never called me back,’’ she explained. ‘‘One didn’t get back to me for two weeks and then told me his schedule was full until after Christmas. So I guess I expected the same from you.’’

Casually, Jake slipped a tanned hand into the pocket of his jeans. ‘‘I just got my business off the ground officially about six months ago. I’ve been consistently busy, one project turning into the next. I’m finishing up a house near Espanola. I can fit you in, probably start next week—Tuesday, since Monday’s Labor Day.’’

"That would be terrific! In a few weeks I won't want to deal with noise and dust—" She stopped. Jake certainly didn't want to hear about her life. He'd come to give her an estimate.

It had been his kindness she'd remembered most about him, his ease with anyone he talked to. Now it wrapped itself around her as he asked, "Is something special happening in a few weeks?"

She only hesitated a heartbeat. "I'm going to become a mother."

At that, his gaze appraised her flowing turquoise-and-rust pants outfit. It molded to her when she moved and clung flatteringly to her figure when she didn't. She became hot under Jake's perusal and was quick to say, "Oh, I'm not having the baby. I mean, not naturally. I'm adopting."

"An infant?"

"Yes. It's a private adoption. A young unwed mother."

Obviously sensing her excitement, he smiled. "And you can't wait?"

"No, I can't wait. I want everything to be in order…everything to be perfect. I've waited for this for so long—" Her voice broke, and she was embarrassed by the depth of feeling in it. Her divorce from Dave and the reasons for it had almost destroyed her. But she'd made a new start.

"You never married?" Jake asked, as if it was an everyday question.

They weren't strangers, after all. She'd worked with Nina at a pottery outlet her last two years in high school, and that's how she'd known Jake. Well, not yed the medicine cabinet she'd purchased and the ighting fixture that would hang above it. She wanted uality, and that didn't surprise him about Tori, either. He'd looked up her art gallery—Perceptions—in the phone book last night after she'd left her message. It was located on Old Santa Fe Trail. She must be doing well if she could afford this little gem of a house. Real estate in Santa Fe was over the top.

''The closet is in here.'' After she led him to the second bedroom, she opened a closet door. Like the rest of the house—except for the kitchen and bathroom—the room had a hardwood floor, but it was expectantly empty. ''I'd like shelves in the upper portion of this closet and a bar for hangers below.''

She pointed to patches of plaster near the floorboards that had crumbled. ''Can you fix that, too?''

''Thanks to apprenticing with my uncle since I was bout ten, I can do a little bit of everything. I have ny general building license and one in ceramic tile, arble and teffazzo.''

She looked impressed. ''You worked with your un- e before you entered the police academy.''

''You have a good memory.''

''I think I remember everything you told me on m night.''

Then, as if she'd revealed a secret, she pinkened in and changed the subject. ''How long do you k this will take? Barbara's baby is due at the end September.''

If my estimate meets with your approval, I'll work st as I can. The job will probably take four or five .''

really *known* him. He'd been four years older and out of her universe.

Except for that one night—a night in Camelot. ''I was married for a while. But it didn't work out. I took back my maiden name after my divorce.''

''Raising a child on your own won't be easy.''

She was tired of hearing that—from her mother, from the media, from her inner doubts. ''Raising a child on my own will be a lot easier than doing it with a man I can't expect to stay, can't expect to trust, can't expect to be an equal partner.''

Jake's brows arched. ''Sorry if I hit a nerve. But I've seen my sister struggle with her two boys since her husband died.''

His remark spiked through the tension. ''I'm so sorry! Nina and I lost touch years ago. I didn't even know she was married. And now she's a widow. Did you say she has boys?''

He grinned. ''Twins. Whirlwinds who don't let me rest a minute when I'm with them. Once in a while I take them for the day. Working from dawn to dusk for a week is easier and requires less energy.''

Although his tone was wry, she could tell he was fond of his nephews. Curiosity urged her to ask, ''You don't have children of your own?''

His mouth straightened into a serious line. ''No. I've never been married and I never expect to be.''

It was an uncompromising statement with feeling behind it that Tori understood. After Dave left, reinforcing childhood doubts and fears that had come into play when she'd decided to get married, she'd known that she'd never trust a man again. Whatever had fueled Jake's remark came from a place deep inside him, a place that had been long established.

The silence between them crackled with awareness. Or was it only her old crush on Jake Galeno deluding her into thinking the attraction she'd always felt for him might now be more than one-sided?

She had no intention of finding out.

A car horn beeped at the curb next door, giving her an excuse to break eye contact as she glanced out the window. ''I'd better show you the problems out back first. We can go through the kitchen.''

Leading the way, she didn't risk another look into those sable eyes that still had the power to fascinate her.

The sky was almost violet, the clouds gray puffs tinged with pink, as Jake stood on Victoria Phillips's patio, focusing on the weather-and-wear damage to the house's exterior northern wall—trying to focus on *it,* rather than her. When he'd heard her message last night, he'd been transported into the past as if he'd stepped into a time machine. She'd always been a beauty with her honey-gold sleek hair, her blue-green eyes, curves that for a few moments had fit so well against his hard body. He'd met her when she'd just turned seventeen and he'd been twenty-one. When he'd taken her to the prom a year later because her date had landed in the hospital with appendicitis, he'd put a leash on his desire. He felt duty bound to protect her innocence.

She was still off-limits. His life was too undecided. He wasn't sure he'd be staying in Santa Fe. He could

end his unpaid leave of absence from the Al
police force with one phone call. But he had
tion of returning to negotiations team work
had no intention of involving himself with
like Tori. Up until a year ago, he'd been an
reading people. If the skills he'd honed since
a kid counted for anything, he was sure Tori
would put the child she wanted to adopt before
affair.

The breeze carried the scent of Tori's perf
deep flowery scent, as he ran his hand over the
on the wall that needed attention. Straighten
caught her watching him, and the sharp stirrin
sire made him take a deep breath.

Damn! He should turn this job down. But h
ling business needed the income. He didn't
deplete the savings he'd worked so hard to
late. ''You mentioned ceramic-tile work, a
cabinet you'd like to have installed and sh
bedroom closet?''

Under the glow of the day-end sun, her c
ened a bit. ''I'll show you.'' Quickly, she
into the house toward the bathroom.

He could see that the ceramic tile-work
the tub and sink would be extensive. ''
you don't want to use a laminate?'' he a
explained everything he'd need to do a
would make.

''I like the permanence of tile—w
right,'' she added with a small laugh.

''Age has something to do with it,
as he ran his finger over the crumbli

"That's great. I'll have about three weeks to get everything ready."

She started across the room and then stopped. "I forgot to show you the breaks in the fence out back."

"I saw them. I'll put the numbers on paper tonight. I can drop it in the mail or give you a call."

"You can just call me."

"You might want to see everything itemized."

"I trust your estimate will be honest."

Her words took him by surprise. "Why is that?"

"Because I doubt if you've changed from the young man who took me to the prom. You could have taken advantage of me that night, and you didn't."

That night he'd seen the stars in her eyes and known she'd thought of him as one of those rescuing knights that had been painted on the paper taped to the walls of the banquet hall. Yes, he could have taken advantage of her.

"You think because I was a gentleman on prom night I won't overcharge you?" His tone was amused.

She laughed. "I'll be able to tell from your estimate. And, Jake...I'm not as naive anymore."

He wondered if that was some kind of warning. "I'll remember that."

Leaving the bedroom, he crossed to her front door and opened it.

Tori came up behind him like an angel who moved with no effort at all. "If you talk to Nina or see her, please give her my regards. Maybe she and I can have lunch together sometime."

"I'm sure she'd like that. I'll tell her."

With a last look at the woman Tori Phillips had become, he left her house, hoping taking this job wasn't a mistake.

When the phone rang the following evening at about eight, Tori wondered if Jake had forgotten something. He'd called earlier with his estimate and she'd given him the go-ahead. Now, she recognized the voice on the other end of the line immediately.

"Tori? It's Nina."

"Nina! How are you? Jake told me about your husband. I'm so sorry."

There was a momentary pause. "It was a shock. But we're managing now. Shortly after it happened, Jake was…at loose ends. It's one of the reasons he came back to Santa Fe, and I'm grateful. The boys need him around."

"I'm glad he could be here for you. How long were you married?"

"Eight years. We…we didn't have the best marriage."

Silence fell over the line, and Tori didn't know what to say to that. Nina had always been very open, and she could tell they'd fallen into the old camaraderie they'd shared as soon as she'd picked up the phone. "Jake tells me you have twins."

"And you're going to adopt a baby! I'd love to catch up with you."

"We could go to lunch someday this week."

"I have a better idea. Why don't you come to dinner tomorrow night? You can meet my boys."

"I don't want to put you to any trouble."

"It's no trouble. Mama does some of the cooking. The guy I'm dating will be here, and so will Jake."

"Jake?"

"Yeah, he likes a good meal a couple of times a week. Did you two talk about old times?"

"There weren't that many. He only took me to my prom."

"You two used to talk when he came into the store."

"That was rare."

"I guess he'd just finished at the academy then. He rose through the ranks fast. I just wish..."

Tori wondered why Nina stopped. "You wish what?"

"Did he tell you what happened? Why he came back to Santa Fe?"

"No. But then, he wasn't here for a social visit, Nina. He came to look at the work I need to have done. Why *did* he come back to Santa Fe?"

"I'd better let him tell you about all that. He doesn't like it when I talk about his life."

"Are you sure he won't mind me coming to dinner? I mean, he might not want to mix his professional life with his personal life."

"You're *my* guest. And as far as Jake's concerned, it wouldn't hurt if his personal life and his professional life got a little mixed up. He has no sense of purpose right now. That was one thing my brother always had."

This baby was going to give Tori's life the purpose and meaning *she* needed. She loved her work at the gallery—promoting artists, finding new ones and giving them a start. But she didn't feel she was put on this earth to simply work and to make a comfortable life for herself. She wanted to be a mother so badly that tears came to her eyes whenever she thought about it. The car accident she and Dave had been involved in had destroyed her chances to conceive a child naturally. But she had no doubt that she could love the baby she'd seen on that sonogram with all her heart.

"Purpose is important," she agreed now. "You can give me the real scoop about motherhood, and everything I'll need to buy that I haven't even thought about."

"It will be so good to see you again, Tori."

"I'm looking forward to it. Just give me the time and directions to your home."

The sun streamed brightly over San Felipe Avenue the following evening as Tori found Nina's house and turned into the driveway. A blue-and-tan truck was parked there already, and Tori recognized it as Jake's.

Picking up the box on the seat beside her—she'd stopped at her favorite chocolatier this afternoon, hoping the assortment of candies would be something everyone would enjoy—she took a deep breath and readied herself to see Jake again.

However, as she rang the bell and waited on the pink concrete porch, she was unprepared for the astonishment on Jake's face when he saw *her.*

Spying the box of candy in her hand, appraising her claret pants and top, he put two and two together. "Nina invited you to dinner?" His tone was neutral.

"Yes. I assumed she'd tell you. I—"

Shoving her brother aside none too gently, Nina appeared in jeans and a purple-checked blouse, spotted Tori and managed to tug her inside, hugging her at the same time. "It's so good to see you."

Nina was a petite version of her brother, feminine in every way he was masculine. Her black hair was still long and straight. Except for a facial line here and there, she didn't look much different than she had at eighteen.

Pulling Tori into the small living room that seemed overcrowded with people, she reintroduced Tori to her mother, Rita Galeno, who had aged considerably. In her mid-fifties now, her hair had gone completely gray and she still wore it in an oblong bun pinned at the back of her head.

She smiled at Tori. "I remember you. You were the one who convinced Nina her eyes were too pretty to wear all that mascara and eyeshadow on them."

A sandy-haired man with twinkling blue eyes who had moved closer to Nina after she'd hugged Tori, now circled Nina's waist with his arm. "You used to wear all that goop?"

Nina laughed. "I was young, defiant and knew all I needed to know. Until Tori came along. Tori, this is my...friend, Charlie Nexley."

"He's not her friend," a child of about five piped up. "He's her *boy*friend."

"Ricky," Nina warned the child, who was obviously the identical twin of the boy standing not far from his elbow.

"We saw them smooching," his brother said with a solemn nod.

When Nina's face flushed, Jake stepped in. Crouching down, he wrapped an arm around each boy's shoulder. ''Ricky, Ryan, this pretty lady is Ms. Phillips. Your mom and I knew her a long time ago.''

''When you were a kid?'' Ryan asked innocently.

Jake chuckled. ''Not quite that long ago. Now, why don't we go out back and get out of everybody's hair?'' Without another look at Tori, Jake stood and ushered the boys to the back door.

Without Jake's presence in the room, Tori felt a definite decrease in tension. She offered the box of candy to Nina. ''Here's something for everybody's sweet tooth.''

''You didn't have to do that.''

Charlie accepted the box and said with a grin, ''I'd better put this out of sight. At least until the boys have had their dinner.''

Nina gave him a grateful smile.

As Charlie moved into the kitchen, Rita pushed herself up from the recliner. ''I'd better check on the soup.''

Nina winked at Tori. ''Tomato and rice with lots of green chilies. She smothered the chicken in roasted hot peppers, too. I hope you're up for it.''

''It sounds delicious.'' Tori placed her purse on a small pine table just inside the door. ''Nina, thanks for inviting me today. But...Jake acted as if he didn't know I was coming.''

''He didn't.''

An uncomfortable silence stretched between the two women until Tori broke it. ''Do you think that's fair to him? He might not have wanted a stranger—''

"You're no stranger. He probably thinks of Charlie as more of a stranger than you. If I had told him you were coming, he might not have come himself. There's something in his voice when he talks about you that makes me think..." She grinned. "Maybe there are a few sparks?"

Tori wasn't going to admit to anything. "Maybe your imagination is working overtime."

Nina studied Tori for a moment, then shook her head. "Nope. I know what I see. The truth is, Tori, I asked you here because Jake needs help."

Tori couldn't imagine Jake Galeno needing anything from anyone. He'd always seemed so confident and self-contained. "What kind of help?"

"I don't know. That's the problem. He doesn't, either. Something happened in Albuquerque that he can't get over. It had to do with his work. He needs to talk about it, but he won't. He needs to get past it, but he can't. He needs to get on with his life, and he says he's doing that, but he's not. I just thought inviting you tonight might get him to open up a bit. He's only his old self when he's with the boys. Maybe you can remind him who he used to be."

"Maybe I'll only make things worse."

"That won't happen. C'mon. You can watch while I make the salad."

While Nina worked and talked, Tori couldn't help but glance out the window often. Jake didn't look like a man who needed help. He was roughhousing with the twins, laughing with them, playing catch. Even when he was young, she'd sensed a deep control about him, an integrity that told everybody he knew who he was and what he could do. That was still the essence of his appearance. But what was going on inside? What had happened in Albuquerque?

She shouldn't care. She wouldn't care.

She'd learned when she was very young that men didn't stay. She'd been nine when her father had walked out on her mother because he'd fallen in love with someone else. She'd seen her mother's tears, pain and depression. She'd seen her father's second marriage break apart, until she'd lost track of him and his second, third and fourth wives. When Tori had married after college, she decided her marriage would be different. It might have been if fate hadn't intervened and changed the course of her life. Dave had walked out on her because she could no longer bear his children.

So much for vows. So much for putting faith and trust in a man. She would never do it again.

As Tori, Nina and her mother discussed their favorite recipes, Charlie went to the carport to check the pressure of Nina's tires. He told her he thought one of them looked low.

Soon after, Nina went to the door and called for the boys to come in and wash up. As they bounded toward the bathroom, Jake entered the kitchen, heading for the sink.

Tori was standing right beside it, boxed in by the counter. The working area of the kitchen was small, and there really wasn't anywhere she could move without looking obvious.

When Jake turned on the spigot, he was close enough to her that she could see the gleam of sweat on his brow and inhale his scent, which seemed to be sunshine and sage and all man. For a moment her senses reeled and she told herself she was being silly. But she couldn't seem to take her gaze from the black hair on his forearms, from the soapy suds slipping over his large hands.

''Catching up?'' he asked as he flipped off the spigot.

It took her a moment to find her voice. ''Sharing favorite recipes.''

''I should have known,'' he said with a smile. ''What else would three women do in a kitchen?''

With a slight shift of his body, he turned toward her. He was so close she could feel his body heat... feel a current of electricity between them immobilize her as she became fascinated by the whorl of hair nestled in the V of his green T-shirt.

He reached behind her, brushing her back. ''I need the towel,'' he explained, his voice husky.

Their gazes locked, and she vividly remembered the moment on her front porch twelve years ago when his arms had encircled her and his head had lowered to kiss her. The smoldering look in his eyes now convinced her he was remembering, too, maybe thinking about what it would be like to kiss her again.

As he lifted the towel from the counter and took a few steps back, she chided herself for being ridiculous.

Finished with the towel, he hung it over the oven door handle. ''Where's Charlie?'' he asked Nina.

''Checking my tire pressure.''

He frowned. ''I was going to do that. In fact—''

Jake never got to finish because the twins ran back into the kitchen. Nina directed them to set the table in the dining area, where she had stacked dishes, silverware and napkins.

Both boys grumbled and groaned.

Ryan protested the loudest. "I want to go outside and watch Charlie."

Jake crooked his finger at them, and they scampered to him, looking up expectantly. "If you help your mom get ready for dinner without complaining, I'll take you for ice cream afterward."

"Carlo's Place?" Ricky asked, wanting to put terms to the deal. "Two scoops?"

"You got it," Jake said with a nod.

As the boys ran to the table, Nina scolded her brother. "That was a bribe."

"Yes, it was. But I figured it was a small price to pay so they didn't argue with you for the next ten minutes."

"Sometimes you have to stand on principle," Nina grumbled.

"Getting things done is better than principle," Rita insisted. "After all, your brother's the expert at negotiation."

At Rita's remark, a smothering hush fell over the kitchen.

Tori glanced from sister to brother to mother, not understanding the sudden tension and the somberness that seemed to have taken over Jake's whole demeanor.

"Jake, I'm sorry," his mother said, looking upset. "I didn't mean—"

"I know you didn't," Jake said quietly. "Forget

about it. I'm going to see if Charlie found the tire gauge.''

Then Jake Galeno exited the kitchen, leaving Tori with unsettling questions she didn't think Nina or Rita were going to answer.

Chapter Two

Dinner with the Galenos was an adventure, Tori decided, as she sat between Jake and Ricky. She made herself concentrate on the twins—that was easier than dealing with the attraction she still felt for Jake—and paid attention to everything they did. Maybe she'd learn something about parenting as she watched Nina interact with them.

When Ricky spilled his milk, it ran off the table and onto Tori's thigh. Nina was much more upset than she was.

Ricky looked upset, too, as if he was ready to cry, until Tori smiled at him. "Milk will wash right out." She gave him her napkin. "Come on, help me mop it up."

While he scurried to wipe the drips on the chair, she helped Nina with the table. She caught Jake watching her and wished she knew what he was thinking. Then again, maybe she didn't *want* to know. Every time his arm grazed hers, every time he reached for a platter or serving dish, she was much too aware of his scent, as well as his sheer physical presence. Surely she didn't still have a crush on him after all these years! Maybe these vibrations were what dating experts called chemistry? If so, she'd never experienced it before…except when she was a teenager and Jake was anywhere within ten feet of her.

After dinner, in spite of Nina's and Rita's protests, Tori helped clean up. She wasn't the type to sit while others worked. When they'd finished in the kitchen, they joined the men on the patio.

Ricky pulled on Jake's arm. "When are we going for ice cream?"

"We just had dinner," Jake replied with a grin.

"I saved room," Ricky insisted, then looked at Tori. "Are you coming, too?"

"Oh, I don't know…" she began.

Approaching her chair, Ricky wheedled, "Uncle Jake says it's the best ice cream in Santa Fe. Mom and grandma won't come because they say they'll get fat if they eat it."

When Ryan added, "Please come," she looked into their dark-brown eyes and couldn't refuse.

"Only if it's all right with your uncle Jake."

A glance at Jake told her nothing. "Of course you're welcome to come." His face was perfectly blank, and his eyes reflected none of his thoughts.

Carlo's Place was a few blocks away—a small, brown stucco building with two parking spaces.

"Most of his customers are within walking distance," Jake explained as if reading her thoughts.

The bench seat of Jake's truck had seemed much too intimate during their drive here.

After the boys unfastened their seat belts in the back, Jake helped them out. His truck's running board was high off the ground.

"If you wait, I'll give you a hand," he offered.

The last thing she wanted was Jake's skin pressed against hers. "I'm fine."

She proved it by sliding to the edge of her seat and then hopping down as gracefully as she could. She thought she saw a knowing smile play on Jake's lips, but couldn't be sure because it was gone too quickly.

Ten minutes later they were sitting at a round redwood table with a striped yellow-and-white umbrella. The boys' cones were dripping all over their hands, but Jake was ignoring that, so Tori did, too.

Leaning close to her, Jake murmured, "I have those wet-wipe things in the truck. I wouldn't go anywhere without them."

She smiled. "I imagine most kids are messy with ice-cream cones."

With a quick half shrug, he remarked, "Don't know. I just know these two can make a mess of whatever they get into." Looking her squarely in the eye, he asked, "Are you ready for that?"

She didn't hesitate. "Yes. More than ready. I've wanted children for years."

"Your husband didn't?"

Confiding in Jake would create a bond between them that Tori didn't want. It was better if she kept her distance, better if she let the attraction between them sizzle and burn out. ''It's a long story.''

With a penetrating look, Jake sat back and gave his attention to his ice-cream cone, stretching his legs out under the table. The swirl of his tongue on the dessert sent a shiver up Tori's back.

After he lazily licked chocolate from his lips, he acknowledged, ''I guess everybody has one of those stories.''

An awkward stretch of time settled between them as cars sped up and down the street. Ricky and his brother took licks from each other's cones as dusk settled in and began to envelop the city.

Finally Jake asked, ''What did you think of Charlie?''

She'd caught Jake watching Charlie carefully more than once. ''I didn't spend much time talking with him. Nina likes him a lot. He seems good with the boys.''

Jake frowned. ''She's only been dating him for two months. I just met him last weekend when she invited him to Sunday dinner.''

''And?''

''I don't know. Today you can't be too careful, that's all. He's a car salesman, and there's nothing wrong with that. I just hope he's not handing her a line. I can't believe she's ready to jump right in so soon after Frank.''

''Maybe she feels the boys need a father figure.''

''They have me.''

Jake's arm was almost touching hers. Tori sat back

and gave him a sideways glance. "Nina's afraid you aren't going to stay in Santa Fe. Are you?"

He finished his cone and wiped his fingers on a napkin. "I don't know. But no matter where I am, I'll be part of their lives."

After she took the last bite of her own cone, she wiped her lips. Just then Jake turned toward her, and his gaze lingered where she'd wiped. Feeling hot, bothered and unsettled, she asked, "Why did you come back to Santa Fe?"

The question brought his gaze to hers. Two cars zoomed up the street before he answered her. "I had to get out of police work for a while. I like working with my hands. I've done that for years, mostly on weekend projects for friends. I find peace in it, and I need that now."

Tori had always admired his honesty. She had the feeling Jake was living in the moment, not knowing what was going to happen next. She'd done that after her divorce.

"Speaking of working with ceramic tile," he said, changing the subject easily, "have you picked out what you want to use yet?"

She shook her head. "I can do that this week. The thing is, I'd love to use hand-painted tiles. I know it would be expensive to use them everywhere, but I hoped I could find some to use as accents here and there. I haven't had a chance to look into it, though."

"I know someone who does hand-painted work. He lives in Taos. If you'd like to see what he has to offer, we could drive up there on Saturday afternoon. Can you get away?"

"I have one full-time assistant and someone who helps part-time. Let me check with them. If they can both work, I'll take the day off."

The twins had finished their cones now, too, and were jabbing each other with sticky fingers, squealing and jumping from their chairs to play tag around the table.

"Okay. It's time to put a lid on it," Jake announced. He motioned to the truck. "Let's move on out. Don't touch anything until I wipe your hands."

Without the complaining Tori expected, Ricky and Ryan looked up at their uncle, then raced to his truck.

Jake's expression was affectionately patient.

As Tori followed Jake and the boys, she noticed again how Ricky and Ryan adored him. Why had he never married and become a father?

When Tori's telephone rang Saturday afternoon, she wondered if Jake was calling to tell her he'd be delayed or couldn't go to Taos. After their trip to Carlo's Place, he'd become quiet, more remote. A little voice full of common sense told her that was best. If they got to know each other better…

However, picking up the phone, she heard Barbara Simmons's voice.

"Hi! Tori?"

"How are you?" Tori asked, always glad to hear from the teenager, yet always fearful, too.

Once Barbara signed the consent papers to give up her parental rights, her decision was irrevocable. She understood that and had asked the court to allow Tori to act as the baby's legal guardian for sixty days before she signed the final papers. In essence, Tori would become the parent, but not officially. She'd agreed to those terms because Barbara was an intelligent, sensitive young woman, just trying to do what was best for her and her baby. And once Tori had seen that baby's picture on the sonogram, she'd fallen in love with him. She had wanted to be a mother so badly, she was willing to take this risk.

"I gained another two pounds," Barbara almost wailed. "Dr. Glessner said it's okay, but I have to get it all off afterward. I'll only have three months. I don't want to be fat when I go to college."

"You've been officially accepted for the winter term?"

"Yes. The letter came last week. Mom and I have been shopping for everything I'll need."

Just as Tori had been shopping for baby supplies. Her closet was full of them, and she couldn't wait to get the baby's room ready. As soon as Jake did the closet and patched the plaster, she could paint.

Her doorbell rang.

Carrying the cordless phone with her, she opened it. Her heart fluttered. Jake looked incredibly sexy in a beige polo shirt and jeans.

Still, she concentrated on Barbara as she motioned him inside.

"I just wanted to tell you," Barbara went on, "that the doctor said everything's A-okay. I can't wait to get this over with. I can hardly see my feet."

In a few weeks, she would be bringing Barbara's baby home. "Keep me up to date on how you're doing. You know I like your progress reports. And stop by if you want to talk.'' It was better to know than to guess exactly what Barbara was thinking about everything.

Whenever she talked to Barbara, fear crept into Tori's heart—fear that the young woman would change her mind, that she wouldn't go through with the adoption. It was a worry Tori couldn't put out of her head.

After she said goodbye to Barbara, she pushed the worry aside and smiled at Jake. She remembered again how good he was with his nephews, how much he enjoyed them.

Then she breathed in the scent of his spicy aftershave and forgot about his nephews. ''I just have to grab my purse. Would you like something to drink before we go?''

He shook his head. ''I told Luis we'd be there around two. We'd better get going.''

A few minutes later Tori was sitting beside Jake in the truck and awkwardness hung between them. Jake's remote attitude gave her the feeling he didn't want to make this trip with her, even though he'd suggested it. ''You know, Jake, if you'd given me the directions, I could have driven up here myself.''

''Luis's place isn't easy to find.''

''I can follow directions and I can read a map.''

''Some women don't like to go to strange places by themselves.''

''And some women don't mind. I guess I'm one of them.''

At that he glanced at her. ''You're as independent as Nina.''

"Is that a compliment?"

A smile twitched the corner of his lip. "Yeah, I suppose. Independent women are just thorny to deal with sometimes."

"As are remote men," she returned before she could stop herself.

The hum of the truck's engine filled the cab as the tires ate up the distance to Taos. Tori stared out the window. She never tired of the Southwest's beauty, a beauty that seemed to change with each passing mile, with the angle of the sun, with the time of the day.

The mountains up ahead were cloaked in sunlight, and streams of it played over peaks and valleys, brush and earth. Sometimes Tori yearned to wrap herself in the scenery and just let the landscape of the yucca, sage and piñon beat through her in primitive rhythms. As old as the land, the vibrations were the same kind of primitive rhythms that thrummed through her with Jake only a couple of feet away.

Except for a glance at her every once in awhile, a flip of the switch to start the tape on the truck's cassette player, Tori thought Jake was lost in his own world.

Finally he asked, "Was that the mother of the baby you're going to adopt on the phone? I couldn't help overhearing."

It seemed funny discussing this with Jake. She hadn't really discussed the adoption with anyone but her lawyer and her mother. "Yes, her name's Barbara. She was accepted for the winter term of college and is looking forward to it."

"When's her due date?"

"September twenty-ninth."

"And then you'll be a mother." The way Jake said it made her think he was reminding himself of that.

Because her worries were so very tied up with her joy, she murmured, "Not exactly."

"What do you mean?"

"Once Barbara signs the papers, her decision is irrevocable. But she's smart enough to understand that feelings aren't something you turn on and off like a water spigot, so she asked for a sixty-day grace period. I'll be legal guardian as soon as the baby's born, but Barbara won't have to make the final decision for sixty days."

"You agreed to that?" There was concerned amazement in the question.

"I don't know how to explain this, Jake, but I can't imagine any woman giving up her baby and not having doubts. I don't want to adopt a baby and then have some kind of war afterward because the mother changes her mind. I want Barbara to be absolutely sure about what she's doing. If those sixty days will do it, then I'm prepared for life to be a little uncertain for that amount of time."

"But what if you've cared for this baby and Barbara *does* change her mind?"

"I don't believe that will happen. I wouldn't have agreed to this if I thought it might. She wants to be a doctor. Her mother wants her to be a doctor. Her mom's divorced and won't accept care of Barbara's baby. She won't even help her with it, because she believes Barbara will be destroying her future if she keeps it. Barbara does, too. She chose me out of fifteen women. She cared about every aspect of the social worker's report. The judge understood that she's a conscientious teenager who wants the best for everybody involved."

"I still think you're taking quite a risk."

"Maybe I am. But motherhood is a risk, no matter how it happens." Now she had a question for him. "Do you want kids someday?"

He was silent for a few very long heartbeats, and then he answered firmly, "That isn't going to happen."

Why? was on the tip of her tongue. Yet she didn't let it slip off. If she knew why, that meant they would be getting to know each other much better. If she knew why, she'd be delving into the part of Jake's life he kept guarded. If she asked why, she had the feeling he wouldn't tell her, anyway.

The sun's brilliance made the landscape dance with golden light. It played over the cottonwoods along the Rio Grande. It flowed over the mountains, outlining a ramshackle house here, a small adobe there. And then there was nothing but land and scrub and piñon. Mountain crests seemed to envelope them, only to disclose higher crests, pink earth, more turquoise sky.

Their conversation was minimal after that, and Tori tried to ignore the movement of Jake's strong, tanned, hair-roughened arms as he guided the steering wheel. His eyes didn't leave the road now, and she wondered if he thought of her as a woman with more optimism than sense.

When they entered the boundaries of Taos, they passed a few fast-food restaurants. Jake took several side roads then, finally weaving between a few houses surrounded by coyote fence. He stopped at a tan adobe *casita* with an Open sign taped to a screen door that rattled in the wind.

"Luis told me he has plenty of tile in stock. Unless of course you want something terrifically unusual. I told him that wasn't likely since you wanted to get the work done quickly."

Forty-five minutes later, Jake loaded boxes of tiles into the back of his truck, thinking about the ones Tori had chosen. She'd seemed enthused about Luis's painting. But then, that shouldn't surprise him. One of the things Jake remembered about Tori was how she became excited over even very small pleasures—colors melting together in a rug, the turquoise-and-coral necklace her mother had given her to wear on her prom night, the Camelot-theme decorations in the hotel ballroom.

And today he'd caught her gazing at the mountains and known she was appreciating their color, their texture, their majesty.

Slamming the tailgate closed on the truck, he decided that being anywhere around her was a mistake. This trip today had been a mistake. After a year, he'd finally found a balance for his emotions, and he didn't want that balance disrupted by desire that couldn't be satisfied, beauty that was out of his reach, a woman who'd captivated him as a teenager and now even more so as an adult. He was in temporary mode. Tori was about to become a mother. *He* never intended to get married. *She* was the type of woman who deserved vows.

Climbing into the driver's seat, his mood darkened as he caught another whiff of her perfume and noticed the creaminess of her skin where her sleek hair fell against her neck. He turned the key in the ignition.

He'd taken a side road toward the center of Taos when Tori asked, ''Do you have to be back at any special time?''

He certainly wasn't in the mood to prolong this outing, to corral his libido and fight his fantasies. ''Why?''

''There's a church near the Plaza—Our Lady of Guadalupe. There's a painting inside that I just love. I thought maybe we could stop there for a few minutes. Would you mind?''

It had been a while since he'd been in a church, even *before* Marion had died. In his work he'd seen too much of the seedier side of life to think a few prayers could fix anything. When he'd attended Marion Montgomery's funeral, the ritual and ceremony and words from the priest had only made him feel guiltier, as if he didn't deserve to be remembering her with the other mourners.

Tori could read his hesitation. ''It's okay. I can visit another time.''

They were less than three minutes from the church parking lot. He wouldn't deny her such a simple request. ''It's no problem.'' Silently, he made the turn that would take them to Our Lady of Guadalupe.

After they parked, they walked toward the rusty-pink adobe church. Tori headed for a door that took them into a vestibule located to the side of the main building.

Stained-glass windows, shadows and the sacred hush compelled Jake to say, ''Go ahead. I'll wait here.'' As he wandered over to the brochures in a wall rack, he added, ''Take your time,'' although he was hoping she would get her fill in a few minutes and they could be on their way.

He knew the painting she spoke of on the side wall of the church. It portrayed Our Lady of Guadalupe and her appearance to an Indian on a hilltop in Mexico. Golden light shone all around her.

After he'd read every brochure in the holder, after he'd studied the church bulletin, after he'd stared at the stained-glass windows, there wasn't one more thing to occupy him. He wandered toward the doors leading into the church, and he saw Tori—not in a pew near the painting, but rather on the kneeler in the small alcove in back where candles were lit. As she looked up at the statue of Our Lady of Guadalupe, he knew what she was praying for.

Finally she stood, blessed herself and joined him in the vestibule. The dimness of the lights, the hushed silence of a holy place seemed to form a net around them.

''You prayed that Barbara wouldn't change her mind, didn't you,'' he said, his voice husky.

Tori nodded. ''I want what's best for her baby, but I want to be a mother so much it hurts.''

He had no bolstering words for her. He'd been gifted with words *before* he'd sent Marion into the hostage situation. He'd known what to say and how to say it and the best person to say it to. Now words always eluded him when he needed them most.

When he stepped outside into the sunshine, he didn't think he could bear being confined in the truck with Tori again right away. "How would you like to walk up to the Plaza? We can stretch before the ride back."

"Are you sure you have time?"

"I'll make the time."

As they strolled side by side the couple of blocks, hot sun bounced off the pavement. The breeze tossed tendrils of Tori's hair along her cheek. Jake longed to brush them away. He longed to do a hell of a lot more than that.

Taking Tori's elbow, the feel of her skin was soft and almost scorching under his callused fingers. After he ushered her across the street, they took the ramp that led down into the Plaza where huge trees were surrounded with adobe borders and a dark brown cross stood as a memorial to veterans. He was guiding her toward one of the benches when he stopped cold.

"What's wrong?" Tori asked.

The woman coming down the steps from the pavilion looked like Marion's mother, Elaine. She had the same short salt-and-pepper hair, wore the same flowing broomstick skirt.

Then the sun hit her face and Jake realized the woman was a stranger. He felt relieved. He hadn't said two words to Marion's mother since her daughter had been killed, and he'd steeled himself for the confrontation ever since he'd been back in Santa Fe, since that was where the woman lived. He knew the possibility existed they could run into each other—in a mall, in a restaurant, on the street. Even in Taos.

"What's wrong?" Tori asked again.

"Nothing."

Her hand clasped his forearm. "Something *is* wrong."

What was wrong was that the past year hadn't eased his guilt or the memory of what had happened one iota. "I'm fine," he said evenly, wanting Tori to drop it.

"I don't think you are. You're different than you used to be."

That comment snapped his gaze to hers. "Hell, yes, I'm different! And so are you. It's been twelve years, Tori. The police work I did taught me a few things and opened my eyes to others."

"Who was that woman?" she asked.

He realized that when his gaze had riveted on the older woman, Tori couldn't help but notice. "I thought I recognized her, but I was wrong."

"Who did you think she was?"

"Drop it, Tori. Just drop it. I'm going to be doing some work for you. That doesn't give you the right to pry into my life."

When he saw the hurt on Tori's face, he almost apologized. Then he told himself that a wall between them was a good thing. "We'd better get back."

She didn't argue, and he could see that she now wanted to end this outing as much as he did.

Chapter Three

To Jake's dismay, when he arrived at Tori's on Tuesday morning her car was still in the carport. She'd given him a key to her house after their uncomfortable ride home from Taos, and he'd hoped she'd have already left for work when he arrived. But it was only eight o'clock, and he guessed the gallery didn't open until nine.

Instead of using the key, he pressed his finger to the doorbell. He was surprised when, after a couple of minutes, Tori didn't answer. Certainly she'd be up by now. He pressed the bell again. Still no answer.

Maybe she was having a cup of coffee on the back patio and couldn't hear the bell.

Following the narrow pathway around the carport to the back, he saw the patio was empty. Maybe she went for a run as part of an exercise regimen. Maybe she'd walked to a coffee shop or a bakery.

Wherever she was, it didn't matter. He had to get started. The sooner he got this job done, the sooner he'd be out of her life. End of sleepless nights, vivid dreams and heart-stopping urges that made him feel as if he'd been kicked in the gut.

He couldn't remember when a woman had ever made him feel so turned inside out.

Using the key Tori had supplied, he opened her front door. When he called her name, she didn't reply.

Returning to his truck, he took his toolbox out of the back and carried it into the house. He'd set up the saw on the patio. First he'd work on the closet in the baby's room, building and fitting shelves, attaching a low bar that a child could eventually reach. When he'd discussed prefabricated closet organizers with Tori, she'd wanted this done the old-fashioned way. He didn't blame her. The fixtures would be sturdier and last a lot longer. Hopefully he'd finish the closet today and could begin the patch plastering. This job could go into next week when all was said and done.

He was headed down the hall to the baby's room when the bathroom door suddenly opened. Tori stood there with one pink towel wrapped around her head and another fetchingly tucked in at her breasts. The sight of her long, graceful legs made him forget all sense of propriety.

He swore just as she gasped, "Jake!"

"I rang the bell," he managed to say in a low, accusing tone, controlled with a great deal of effort.

"I must have been in the shower. I overslept this

morning and I'm running late. I thought I could get dressed before you arrived.''

''It's after eight.'' He couldn't take his eyes off her. She was clutching both the towel at her breasts and the one enfolding her hair as if her life depended on holding them in place. Almost mechanically he offered, ''If I'm going to be in your way, I can start out on the patio.''

''No. You won't be in my way. But I...'' Her face was red, and turning redder. ''Could you...could you just turn your back until I get into the bedroom? I'm afraid something's going to give way...''

He realized he was waiting for exactly that. If the towel slipped... He kicked himself for being a boor. ''Sure.'' He swiftly turned and faced the living room. ''I didn't mean to barge in on you like this.''

''No problem,'' she said a bit breathlessly as she scurried down the hall to her room. ''It's my fault for not setting my alarm last night. I was writing in my journal until late and I fell asleep.''

As he glanced over his shoulder, he saw she was hidden behind her bedroom door now. Only her head and one shoulder peeked out. The turban had apparently come loose because she swiped that towel away. Her wet hair framed her face. She looked vulnerable, younger than the thirty he knew she was and tempting enough to kiss.

Concentrating on her words rather than his last thought, he said, ''Someone once suggested I do that. Keep a journal. But I couldn't see the point.'' Before he'd decided to take a leave of absence from the police department, he'd had sessions with one of the psychologists.

"Oh, there *is* a point to keeping a journal. It helps me sort things out. It helps me articulate thoughts that haven't completely formed yet. Putting them down on paper somehow releases them from my head and my heart."

Although he knew he shouldn't, he couldn't help closing some of the space between them. "Maybe you just have a talent for it."

She shook her head and her wet hair swung. "It doesn't take talent. It just takes time and…honesty."

That was the crux of the matter. Maybe he knew if he was completely honest with himself, he'd never recover from what had happened in Albuquerque.

As they gazed at each other, the space in the small hall seemed filled with sparks of electricity. He was much too conscious of what she wasn't wearing, of the bed a few feet from her door. How did he get drawn into conversations with Tori that opened up places he wanted to keep closed?

With a great effort he decided that a lighter touch would be best. So he forced a smile. "I'd better get started or I'll still be here when you get home for supper."

Then he went into the baby's room to examine the areas that needed to be plastered. Working with his hands would help him forget about a woman he was thinking entirely too much about touching.

Tori's arms were full of packages when she returned home that evening. As she peeked into the nursery, she saw Jake sweeping debris into a corner. ''I left work a little early. One of the department stores was having a terrific sale on baby clothes.''

All day she'd thought about Jake seeing her barely dressed, the look in his eyes when he had. Her gaze swept the room and the work he'd done. ''It looks great. How soon can I paint?''

''I'll finish the plastering tomorrow. You should give it at least ten days.''

''Barbara's not due for three weeks. I might be able to get it painted and let it air out. I plan to keep the baby with me in my room for the first week, anyway.'' She knew she was babbling, but she was still embarrassed about this morning, and talking kept her less aware of Jake.

''You might not get much sleep. Babies make all kinds of sounds,'' he offered practically.

''I doubt if I'll get much sleep, anyway. We'll see.''

One of the bags in her arms started to slip, and she would have dropped everything if he hadn't strode quickly toward her and taken a few of the bags. He smelled like man, and work, and stirred up sensations she'd kept a lid on for years. When he was this close, all she could think about was kissing him.

''Where do you want these?'' he asked huskily.

Breaking eye contact, she went over to the closet, examining the prepainted shelves he'd installed and the bar securely fastened in the lower section. ''We can put all the bags in there for now.''

She was stacking her purchases on the shelves when he approached with the ones he held. His arm brushed against hers. ‘‘I thought you’d be gone when I got home,’’ she murmured.

‘‘It didn’t work out that way,’’ he said easily, though his eyes had gone almost black, and she glimpsed the fire and intensity there.

She knew both emanated from a place inside Jake that had led him into police work. Why was he working with tile, instead? She decided to go at the conversation sideways. ‘‘I guess you put in less hours now than you did on the police force.’’

His expression became wary. ‘‘I suppose that’s true.’’

‘‘The night of the prom when I asked you why you were going into police work, you said you wanted to make the world a better place. Was that the only reason?’’

As he thought about her question, she held her breath. She needed to know this piece of the puzzle.

Straightening the packages he’d set on the shelves, he finally answered her. ‘‘I became a cop because of my father.’’

Tori hadn’t known anything about Nina’s family when she’d worked with her all those years ago. She’d met her mother once or twice, and back then Rita Galeno had seemed quiet and reserved, maybe even withdrawn. Much different from the way she’d been the other night. ‘‘Your father encouraged you?’’

Jake gave a humorless, short laugh and turned away. ‘‘Not in the way you mean. He was an angry man—angry at the world for the hand it had dealt him. When he drank, the anger would come out. If a meal displeased him, if Nina and I made too much noise, he'd erupt like a volcano.''

''Did you know why he was angry?''

Leaving her standing at the closet, Jake once again picked up the broom. ''Because of me. My mom was pregnant with me and they had to get married. I never saw one happy moment in their marriage. She never stood up to him, never wanted more than she had. I was about twelve when I asked her why she stayed. She was so matter-of-fact about it. She said Dad earned a good living, and she had no education and two children to raise. How could she make it on her own? I came to believe that my father didn't want to be married or responsible for a family, and that's what kept him short-tempered. My mother was always sad because she felt like a hostage.''

''So...why police work? To intervene in domestic disputes?''

This time Jake's answer came more slowly. ''I learned very young that an ounce of prevention is worth a pound of cure. Whenever Dad was volatile, my tone of voice, the right words and a sympathetic ear could defuse his anger. When I joined the police force, I think I did it simply because I wanted to keep peace. Everything I'd learned with my father led me into hostage-negotiation work, and eventually I supervised and was a primary negotiator on the team.''

Supervisor of the negotiations team—the epitome of protection and responsibility. ''Why did you leave?'' she asked quietly.

He kept sweeping. ''It doesn't matter.''

She knew that wasn't true. But it was obvious Jake

was drawing a boundary between them, a boundary that now felt too restrictive.

"Jake..." she began.

Propping the broom against the wall, he approached her, his eyes dark and piercing. "Leave it alone, Tori."

But she couldn't. "Why?"

"Because my life cracked into a thousand pieces and I'm trying to glue it back together. It's a solitary road."

That was another piece of the puzzle she needed to understand him. "You've always chosen the solitary road, haven't you."

"Yes."

Good sense urged her to look away. She knew she shouldn't let desire rise inside her. Most of all, she shouldn't let Jake see it. But gazing into his eyes now, she knew she wanted to touch him. She knew she needed to feel his lips on hers. Maybe she needed to prove that everything she'd remembered about their kiss twelve years ago had been a teenage girl's dream.

"Don't look at me like that," he warned hoarsely.

But she was powerless to turn away. She wanted to taste passion again, even if it was only for a moment.

With a deep groan, Jake took her by the shoulders and bent his head to hers.

Tori had anticipated the kiss, had been longing for it. But he didn't set his lips on hers. Not right away. His tongue outlined them first. She shivered, even more eager for the feel of his mouth. Even in that kiss at eighteen, she'd known Jake was experienced. That experience still showed as he teased her. Then, as if he couldn't stand the torture, either, he finally sealed his lips to hers.

When his hips pressed against hers, her breath caught. He was obviously attracted to her as much as she was attracted to him. His hands left her shoulders as his arms enveloped her, and along with desire, she felt the safety of a strong man's embrace.

She'd never, *ever* experienced anything like this—not the tingling fire in her limbs, not the excitement twirling in her stomach, not the intoxicating knowledge that he wanted her.

Her marriage to Dave had been staid and comfortable—before the accident. What would Jake say if he knew she couldn't have children?

That thought fled with all the others as his tongue coaxed her lips apart and she found herself lost in a land that was as primordial as the high desert, as dizzying as the tallest mountain, as vast as the universe. She melted into him as he securely held her, tempted her, intoxicated her.

Then as suddenly as black clouds gathered over the mountains, Jake pulled away, leaving her standing alone. His eyes were black with turbulence, his face grim with regret. "That was a mistake. It won't happen again." He looked almost fierce in his certainty of that.

Tori strove to put her scrambled thoughts in order, still trembling from the power of the passion that had risen between them. "Because you don't know where you're going?" she asked shakily.

"Because we both have lives that are more complicated than we know what to do with. You're going to be a mother, and that child is going to come first, isn't he?''

She nodded, knowing her life would revolve around her child, knowing there was no room for the doubt and uncertainty a relationship with a man would bring.

''I don't think you're the type of woman who would have the inclination to hop into a man's bed while a baby's crying in the room next door.''

He knew her, maybe even better than she knew herself. She was usually cautious, analyzing everything three different ways. But the feelings Jake aroused had made her forget caution, and she couldn't do that—especially not with a baby to think of.

She didn't know what to say any more than she knew what to do. There was no reason she should feel like a tongue-tied teenager around Jake, but she felt as naive and vulnerable as she had after his kiss the night of the prom. ''You'll be back tomorrow?'' she asked, looking around the room, wanting to make sure he'd finish the job he'd started.

''I'll be back tomorrow. I'm hoping to finish this by Friday.'' Then he turned and left.

When she heard the door shut, she took one very deep breath, closed her eyes and thought about getting the room ready for her baby.

On Thursday Jake was working in the bathroom when Tori returned home. It was a few minutes before five and she had hoped to catch him still here. They needed to clear the air. Yesterday he hadn't arrived until after she'd left, and he'd been gone before she'd gotten back home. It was fine if that was the way he wanted to play it. But Nina had asked her to go shopping with her on Sunday, and if they renewed their friendship, there was no way Jake was going to be able to avoid her completely.

When she peeked into the bathroom, he was washing down a section of tile. He glanced over his shoulder and her heart sped up when his gaze locked with hers. The kiss and everything she'd felt while he was kissing her hummed through her with vibrations that could still shake her.

He broke eye contact first and continued wiping the tiles. "I'm almost finished here. I'll be out of your hair in a few minutes." His wide-legged rigid stance as he stood in her bathtub told her he was remembering the kiss, too.

"I made stew in the crockpot this morning and it's ready. Would you like some?"

"Tori, I don't think it's a good idea—"

"We need to clear the air. I thought we could talk. It's a bowl of stew, Jake, not a full-course meal." Her attempt to lighten the atmosphere didn't work.

"I need to wash up."

She pointed to the sink. "The soap's in the cupboard underneath. If you really don't want to stay, that's fine. But Nina and I are going to be friends again, it seems, and you and I might run into each other. It would be better if there isn't all this... awkwardness between us."

At her attempt to characterize whatever was between them, the corners of his lips twitched up. "Awkwardness is a new way of putting it." At last he nodded. ''All right. I'll have a bowl of stew with you. I have a clean shirt in the truck.''

A short time later, Jake came to the table in a clean black T-shirt that stretched appealingly over his broad shoulders and hugged the muscles of his upper arms. At that moment Tori almost panicked. Maybe she'd been wrong about this tête-à-tête. Could she learn to be just a casual friend to Jake when her heart always pounded furiously in his presence?

He motioned to the table. ''Looks like more than a bowl of stew.''

She'd bought a fresh loaf of bread on her lunch hour and made a quick salad while he'd washed up.

''Nothing fancy,'' she assured him. ''I would've done the same for myself. Should I make a pot of coffee?''

''No. This is fine.''

It was obvious he didn't want to linger. He'd eat her stew, have the talk and get out of her house as quickly as he could.

Jake waited for her to sit before he lowered himself into his chair. ''It smells good.''

He was making conversation, but she could tell he was on guard.

''My mother's recipe. She used to prepare most meals before she left for work. Then we had more time to spend together in the evenings.''

''It was just you and your mom?''

''My father left when I was nine. My mother went to night school and became a paralegal.''

Something in her voice must have hinted at the hurt still there. ''Are you in contact with your dad now?''

''No. A few years ago I heard he and his fourth wife moved to Missouri.''

''Fourth wife?''

''He falls in and out of love easily. At least, that's what my mother always told me. But I don't think it's love at all. He finds a woman who suits his needs for the moment, and when she doesn't, he moves on.''

After a few spoonfuls of stew, Jake remarked, ''That's the way some people look at marriage.''

''Your parents stayed together.''

''For all the wrong reasons. Their marriage kept them both in a prison. My father's resentment made him mean. From what I can see, marriage is a trap.''

Tori could understand why Jake believed as he did. Yet… ''Maybe if two people marry for the right reason—''

Her phone rang and she murmured to Jake, ''I'll just let the machine take that.'' But a few seconds later when she heard, ''Ms. Phillips, this is Detective Trujillo from the Santa Fe Police Department. The jewelry store a few shops down from yours was robbed this evening and—''

Jumping up from her chair, Tori grabbed the handset. ''Detective Trujillo? This is Tori Phillips. Did someone break into my gallery?''

''We don't think so, ma'am, but we'd like you to come down here and check things over. We'd like to see if your security system was tampered with.''

''I can be there in ten minutes. Should I meet you out front?''

''That will be fine.''

Putting the cordless phone back in its stand, she

looked at Jake. "I'm sorry about this, but I have to go to the gallery. The detective wants me to make sure the thief didn't try to get inside."

"I know Phil Trujillo. We went to the academy in Albuquerque together. Do you want me to come with you?"

"Do you want to?"

"No," he said with a slow smile. It was the one she remembered from so long ago. "But I might be able to get information from Phil that you can't. Detectives investigating a case are tight-lipped."

She had the feeling that Jake was itching to get back into police work, but something was stopping him. Maybe she'd find out what that was tonight. "I'd be glad to have you along. I've never had an almost-break-in before."

"Then let's go see if your security system kept your gallery safe."

Perceptions was located in a small plaza with a string of other shops. Tori's shop, situated at the closed U end of the parking lot, was white stucco and attached to a bakery on the right. On the left, a brick pathway ran parallel to the narrow driveway that led to the rear entrance. There were two police cruisers, their lights still flashing, blocking the entrance to the walkway that wended to Tori's shop, the bakery, and the adjoining building, where the jewelry store was located next to a leather boutique.

Jake and Tori climbed out of his truck, then angled around a cruiser to her gallery.

The detective who was standing at the door, his arms crossed over his chest, recognized Jake immediately. ''Galeno! What are you doing here? Going to join the Santa Fe PD?''

"I was with Tori when she got your call. Just thought I'd come along as a concerned friend to find out what was going on.''

''Not much,'' the detective said. ''We're waiting for the owner of the bakery and that leather shop. Just wanted to make sure nothing else was tampered with. As you can see, we dusted for prints on the knob and around the door. Same thing at the back entrance. But even if we find prints that match any at the jewelry store, that doesn't mean we've found our guy. Shoppers, especially tourists, go from one shop to the next. That right, Ms. Phillips?''

''Yes, it is.'' Taking her key from her purse, she asked, ''Is it all right if I open the door?''

The detective nodded, watching her closely. She noticed Jake was watching her, too, and then she saw why. There were scratches around the keyhole. She didn't know what they were from, but she was pretty sure they hadn't been there earlier when she'd locked up.

She pointed them out to the detective.

''Yeah, we noticed them,'' Trujillo offered. ''We were waiting to see if you said anything. Any guesses as to what they're from, Galeno?''

Phil knew Jake would recognize the scratches. ''Possibly a pick that slipped. But I don't get why he would even attempt the front door.''

''The back door's solid steel, the lock obviously heavy-duty. This one is, too, but it's not quite so cumbersome,'' Tori explained.

''Right on the mark,'' Trujillo said.

Taking a few steps back, Jake studied all the stores in the layout. ''He might've just been making a quick run through here, seeing what was possible and what wasn't. What happened at the jewelry store?''

''This guy doesn't have much finesse. If you walk down there, you'll see he broke the window, set off the alarm, crashed some cases and grabbed what he could. The good stuff was all in the safe, so he didn't get to that. But the store's security service tried to call the owner before they called us, so the unsub—unidentified subject,'' he explained to Tori, ''had time to hightail it out of here. My partner's interviewing everybody he can find within a decent radius. Ms. Phillips, how about if you turn off that alarm system. I'll see if anything's amiss inside.''

Tori opened the door and pressed in the security code. A green light came on. ''It's off,'' she murmured.

Detective Trujillo stepped past her, his hand inside his suit coat, as he ordered, ''Wait here.''

Tori wasn't sure what to think, and she looked up at Jake.

He placed a hand on her shoulder. ''He just wants to make sure this guy is gone…and was acting alone.''

A few minutes later, the detective beckoned them inside, and Tori took a cursory look around, then made a more detailed search. ''I locked up myself tonight a few minutes early. Nothing's been touched.''

She saw Jake studying the pictures on the walls, the sculptures on stands, the case of unique jewelry and pillboxes, the rack with hand-carved walking sticks.

She'd decorated the gallery in the mountain colors of rust, green and blue. It blended with everything she sold, making the ambience of the gallery welcoming, yet sedate, unpretentious, yet undoubtedly exclusive.

Already, Phil Trujillo had opened the door into the room beyond. ''Is this for storage?''

''Yes. Right now it's crammed full of work I'm going to display for Christmas and an artist's opening coming up.''

She hurried after the detective, saying to Jake, ''He needs to be careful with my inventory.''

Jake caught her elbow. ''Phil's no bull in a china shop. He knows what he's looking for.''

Jake's fingers were hot on her skin. ''And that is?''

He shrugged and released her. ''He'll know when he sees it.''

''Are you speaking from experience?''

''Intuition goes a long way in catching a criminal. But so does good eyesight.''

Jake was being flippant now, but the serious expression on his face told her he didn't consider any of this a laughing matter.

''Tell me something,'' Trujillo said as he reentered the gallery. ''Would any of that stuff in there be worth a bundle on the black market?''

Tori motioned to canvases propped against the far wall. ''I have a few artists who are well-known and their work is becoming more scarce. The right word in the right circle of private collectors who don't care about fenced goods, and the thief could set up a nice retirement account.''

''We're assuming this is a man,'' Jake said, ''but

we shouldn't necessarily make that assumption, should we, Phil?''

The detective's eyes became hooded now. He'd shared all the information he'd intended to share. Everything else was not for public consumption. ''I like facts better than assumptions.''

While the two men nosed around, Tori checked the remaining inventory in the storage area, once in a while looking over her shoulder.

Finally she admitted, ''Everything appears fine in here, too.''

''Then there's no reason why you can't return home,'' Trujillo said. ''Let's lock it all up and you can be on your way.''

Ten minutes later, as Jake was driving Tori home, he asked, ''Have you ever thought about putting a security system in your home?''

''I've thought about it.''

''It's like the tile in your bathroom, right? You've been meaning to call somebody sometime, but just haven't gotten around to it?''

''Exactly,'' she admitted as she let out a sigh.

''Do it, Tori. With a baby in the house, you're not going to want to take any chances.''

She glanced over at him. ''I will.''

In her driveway, he didn't switch off the ignition. ''I'll wait until you're inside.''

It was almost dark now. ''Are you sure you don't want to come in and have that bowl of stew?''

''Having supper with you wasn't about the stew in the first place. It was about clearing the air.''

''We haven't done that.''

"I think we have. You want to stay friends with Nina, and you don't want to feel awkward around me. Does that about sum it up?"

That was essentially what she'd said and he'd obviously been listening. "I suppose."

"Look, Tori. There has always been chemistry between us. I stayed away from you when you were seventeen and eighteen because you were too young to handle what I wanted. Now—"

"I'm old enough to handle anything," she interrupted him with spirit.

"Yes, you are. But you're also going to be a mother. Where can a man not interested in a permanent relationship fit into that mix?"

The question was almost a challenge, as if he was daring her to say she wanted a roll in the hay, a quickie in the afternoon at his apartment, a hot, short interlude while her baby slept in the room next door. Of course she couldn't say any of those things. She thought more of herself than that. She thought more of the child she was going to adopt than that. She'd never had a hot affair, and she'd only ever had one relationship—her engagement and marriage to Dave.

Reminding herself that Dave had left, just as her father had left, she replied, "A man doesn't fit into the equation at all."

Then she flipped open the handle on the door and put one foot on the running board. "Thanks for coming along with me tonight, Jake. And for...clearing the air. I'm sure neither of us will feel any awkwardness now."

As she climbed out, slammed the door and hurried up her front walk she heard Jake call, "Tori, wait."

His command echoed in her ear. Still, she ignored it and practically ran inside.

She wasn't about to lose her heart again to any man—not even to Jake Galeno!

Chapter Four

Tori had just slipped on a dress with a peasant top and an ankle-length red, turquoise and yellow skirt the following morning when her phone rang.

After winding the dress's long sash around her waist, she snatched up the receiver. "Hello."

"Tori, it's Jake."

She waited, letting him explain why he was calling.

"I thought it might be a good idea for me to check out your gallery before you opened it this morning."

"Why?"

"To make sure no one got inside last night after the commotion was over."

"You don't think he'd come back..."

"I don't know. But I don't like the idea of you walking in there this morning alone."

Her heart sped up at his concern, but then she reminded herself Jake had been a cop. Making sure anyone was safe was second nature to him. ''I *would* feel safer if you checked out the gallery. I usually park at the rear entrance. Do you want to meet me there?''

''Around eight-forty-five?'' he asked, knowing she usually went in around nine.

''That will be fine. I'll meet you there then.''

A few minutes later Tori brushed her hair, used her curling iron and carefully applied lipstick. Jake Galeno was a complex man who wasn't easy to read or predict, and she shouldn't even think about trying to do either.

When she arrived at the gallery half an hour later, Jake was already standing at the back entrance. He was wearing a gray T-shirt with a V-neck, and jeans that hugged his hips and powerful thighs as if they'd been made just for him.

As she locked her car and crossed to him, she wished she could stop noticing details about him—the way his chest hair filled that V, the way his eyes darkened when he looked at her, the way he kept his expression studiously neutral so she had no clue what he was thinking.

''I have to go in the front so I can turn off the alarm system,'' she explained.

He nodded. ''I know. I was just looking around. I stopped in at the bakery. The woman behind the counter told me they've been doing a brisk business this morning—lots of people curious about what happened last night.''

They walked along the side of the building to the front, where Tori's gaze automatically went to the jewelry store. The front window was boarded up.

"George will probably try to get that replaced today so he can reopen," she murmured.

Turning to the door of Perceptions, she unlocked it, pressed in the code for the security system and then stepped inside.

Jake's hand was on her shoulder to stop her. She could feel the weight and heat and strength of it through her dress.

After he'd taken a quick pass around the gallery, he went into the storage room. She crossed to the computerized cash register, flipped the switch to activate it, pressed another to start a Burning Sky CD and stowed her purse under the counter. Pulling a file folder from the cabinet behind the counter, she opened it and prepared to inventory the shipment that had come in yesterday. Whether Jake was here or not, she had work to do.

Glancing toward the windows that were fitted with special glass to protect the gallery's items from ultraviolet rays, she realized that she hadn't opened the blinds. That was always the first thing she did when the store opened. Obviously she was distracted—by everything that had happened…and by Jake.

Tori heard Jake moving around in the storage room. Wondering what he was doing, she was about to check when the gallery door opened and the security bell dinged. Ready to greet a customer, she turned and saw…Barbara!

The teenager was more than eight months pregnant now and she'd gained about twenty-five pounds. She'd been uncomfortable with the weight gain right from the beginning. Her brown hair had been lightly frosted before her pregnancy but hadn't been dyed since, because of the baby. Tori could see now that Barbara had had her hair cut in a short pixie style that became her.

"You're out and about early," Tori said. "I like your hair."

Barbara ran her hand through the short cut. "I just had it done this morning. I thought it would be better for…everything that's coming up."

Tori could see that Barbara had something on her mind. "Your new life at college?"

"No. Yes. I mean, well…I've seen pictures of women in labor and their hair always looks a mess. I thought maybe if mine was short, I might not look so bad."

"Nobody's going to care how you look."

"I care." Frowning, Barbara moved to a burgundy leather club chair, one of the few Tori had positioned in the gallery for her customers.

Lowering herself into it, Barbara looked up at Tori with wide, blue eyes. "I've been worrying about all of it. I wake up in the middle of the night thinking about delivering this baby. I'm scared to death about labor and all the pain. What if I can't handle it? What if in the middle of it, I just can't do it?"

Crossing to the young woman, Tori dropped to a crouch beside the chair. "Have you spoken to your doctor about your concerns?"

Barbara nodded. "Dr. Glessner answers all my questions. She knows I want to try to do it naturally—that's what's best for the baby. But that's what I'm most afraid of. What if I just can't do it? What if I have to take drugs and they hurt the baby?"

Tori felt at a total loss, never having gone through

the experience herself. She'd read about it, heard about it and had always desperately wanted to experience it. But she never would.

A deep, calm, male voice assured Barbara, "My sister had twins and she did it naturally. The biggest part of the secret is in the breathing. Have you gone to any classes?"

When Barbara spotted Jake, she glanced at Tori curiously.

Tori made the introductions, adding, "Jake's sister, Nina, and I were friends in high school."

As Jake approached Barbara, she sat up a little straighter. Her eyes became wider. Tori realized Barbara was noticing that Jake was a very rugged, appealing man.

The teenager smiled at him, then admitted, "I...I didn't take any classes because they're not just about learning how to breathe. They're about being a parent, too, and since I'm giving Tori the baby..."

Jake. seemed to understand Barbara's dilemma. "My sister, Nina, has a memory to envy. My guess is she still remembers the breathing exercises and anything else she learned. She might even still have the books on the subject. She read everything about labor, delivery and babies she could find before Ricky and Ryan were born."

Never shy, Barbara asked, "Do you think I could talk to her? I don't know anyone else who went through it. My mom's no help at all. She said they gave her lots of drugs. And I don't want that."

"Nina and I were going to go shopping on Sunday. Let me give her a call," Tori suggested. "Are you free Sunday afternoon to meet us?"

"What else would I be doing?" Barbara grumbled. "I don't exactly have a social life anymore."

The door to Perceptions opened once more, and the bell rang again.

Barbara pushed herself out of the chair. "I've taken up enough of your time." She looked up at Jake. "Thanks for telling me about your sister."

"No problem," Jake said kindly. "If Nina can help you, she will."

Tori laid her hand on Barbara's shoulder. "Nina works till five. I'll call her this evening and then get back to you."

As Barbara headed for the door, Tori stepped around a sculpture on a pedestal to greet her customer, then broke into a wide smile. "Peter! It's so good to see you. When did you get into town?"

Jake found himself watching with interest as Tori crossed the gallery to greet the man who'd just come in. She gave him an exuberant hug. Jake didn't like the churning in his gut as he watched the two embrace. The guy looked to be about forty. He was about six feet, *GQ* handsome and dressed in a crisp, collarless, pin-striped shirt and casual charcoal slacks. He obviously knew Tori well enough to hold her close and kiss her on the cheek.

The stranger's smile was all for Tori. "I got in last night, much too late to call you. Do you have time to talk now about framing the canvases and finalizing the details of the brochure for the show?"

There was a familiarity between the man and Tori that irritated Jake. His perfect white teeth and charming smile made Jake clench his jaw. Hadn't he decided that walls between him and Tori were a good thing?

Hadn't he decided it was better if they both kept their distance?

Tori glanced at Jake as if she wondered how long he'd be staying. Then she introduced him to Peter Emerson.

She didn't explain what Jake was doing in her gallery, just mentioned he was a friend. About Peter, she said, "Peter's one of my stars. I found him last year. We sold out at our first showing."

Jake remembered seeing the canvases with Emerson's name as he looked through her inventory and checked the building for obvious flaws a burglar could take advantage of. There were none. Emerson's paintings, though, wouldn't be hanging in *his* living room.

"I saw some of your work back there." Jake nodded over his shoulder. "You're the artist who paints images in mirrors and lakes and the like." Some of them were downright weird, but then, Jake was no art connoisseur.

"Yes, I do. It's my trademark. Tori saw the promise in it. Since she did, I can take time off to paint, rather than work as an accountant all year and dread tax season."

Emerson and Tori exchanged a look of mutual admiration that Jake found disturbing—as disturbing as her smile, the brush of her hair along her cheek, the curves that were always subtly emphasized by her flowing clothes.

He needed to get back to working with his hands, not pretending he was a detective again. Last night after Phil called Tori, the old adrenaline had kicked in. All his senses had gone on alert. He'd realized he remembered *how* to be a detective. He just didn't think he'd ever *want* to be a detective again.

"I've got to be going," he said now, moving toward the door.

"Jake?" Tori's voice stopped him. "Thanks for coming in with me this morning. I appreciate it."

"No thanks necessary. Your gallery's as secure as it can get without an armed guard. Hopefully, the thug who broke into the jewelry store is on his way somewhere else."

After a nod to Peter, Jake left Tori's gallery, eager to finish the work on Tori's house so that he could find balance in his life once more.

To Tori's dismay, when she, Nina and Barbara arrived at Nina's on Sunday, Nina announced, "I see Jake's here with the boys." Her friend hurried up the steps and threw open the door.

When Tori had called Nina about getting together with Barbara, Nina had insisted Barbara join them when they went shopping. Then they could all have supper together afterward—at Nina's house. Tori had assumed Nina's mom would be taking care of the twins.

"Where's your mom?" Tori asked lightly, wondering if Nina was trying to throw her and Jake together on purpose. If so, it was going to be very awkward.

"She had the chance to spend the day with a friend in Albuquerque, so I asked Jake to take the boys."

Going into the kitchen, Nina looked out the back door. "Uh-oh. Charlie's here, too."

"Uh-oh?" Barbara asked, picking up on Nina's tone. "Don't they get along?"

"They don't know each other yet," Nina said with a sigh. "Jake is protective of me and the twins, and he hasn't decided whether or not he likes Charlie yet. I think it's a territorial thing. Men." She shook her head as she called out the back door. "We're home. Anybody ready to order pepperoni pizza?"

While the boys stayed outside, Jake and Charlie both came into the kitchen. There was obvious tension between them.

With a grim line to his mouth, Charlie said, "I finished working on my car early. I came over and told Jake I could take the boys to the park, and he could do whatever he wanted. But he insisted—"

"I didn't know if you'd want Charlie to take the boys off on his own. We've never discussed it."

"I trust Charlie," Nina told him softly.

"Next time I'll know."

"I promised Ricky and Ryan I'd play catch with them," Charlie said. "If you don't have any objections, I'll do that now." His cool attitude was directed at Jake, and he left the kitchen abruptly, letting the screen door bang shut behind him.

"How was your shopping trip?" Jake asked the three women, apparently not wanting Barbara to feel uncomfortable with the family tensions zipping around her.

Barbara rubbed the small of her back and Tori suggested, "Why don't you have a seat?"

Nina took a pitcher of lemonade from the refrigerator. "We helped Barbara pick out a few outfits for college. It was fun. Made me wish I was ten years younger."

"You're not old," Barbara protested. "You could still go to college if you wanted to."

Tori had been glad to see that Barbara had felt comfortable with Nina right away. Apparently Jake could see that, too.

The teenager turned to him now. "Nina said you were her coach when Ricky and Ryan were delivered."

"Yes, I was. It was an experience I'll never forget."

"My husband was out of town a lot," Nina explained to Barbara. "Mama was no help at all and got all beside herself as soon as I went into labor. She couldn't even find the suitcase I'd packed. Jake was a great coach. He kept me focused and didn't let me give up when I thought I couldn't push another time."

"Just thinking about it scares me to death," Barbara admitted. "My mother doesn't even want to be there." She shook her head as tears came to her eyes. "She acts as if I'm not pregnant. She acts as if I've got the flu and it'll soon be gone. I guess it soon will be," Barbara added wistfully.

It was moments like these when Tori's fears gripped her the hardest.

Jake's gaze locked with hers, and she could see that he knew what was going through her mind. What if Barbara never signed those final consent papers? What if her mother was pushing her to give this baby up, but deep in her heart Barbara didn't want to do it?

"If I find a birthing class like you and Nina recommend, will you be my coach?" she asked Tori.

"I'd be glad to be your coach." Tori couldn't refuse. At this point she had to support Barbara any way she could.

Silence settled over the kitchen for a few moments until Jake broke it. ''The boys were getting hungry. Maybe I should place the order for that pizza.''

After the pizza arrived and they all sat outside at a large picnic table, Tori munched on her slice, observing the family dynamics. She and her mom had led a quiet life after her dad had left. With her mother working long hours at a law office, their time together was limited. Tori had always wondered what it would be like to be part of a large family, to have a sister to share secrets with, a brother to climb trees with. Watching the twins' antics, as well as Nina trying to keep peace between Jake and Charlie while also trying to include Barbara and Tori in all the conversations, Tori felt a sense of belonging overtake her that she didn't understand. Realistically, she didn't belong here with them. Maybe she felt bonds because of her renewed friendship with Nina and her connection to Barbara.

The sense of belonging transformed into something else entirely whenever Jake's gaze met hers. Then she felt as if she'd been stung by something powerful, something she wasn't sure how to handle.

Nina gathered the books she'd collected on childbirth, and Barbara left after finishing her pizza. When the boys ran to their room to get a game, Nina and Charlie talked quietly in the kitchen. Tori found herself alone out back with Jake.

''She's probably trying to unruffle his feathers,'' Jake said almost to himself. He moved to the edge of the deck and stood under the scraggly shade of a piñon pine.

Tori's sandals sounded on the wood planks as she

slid her hands into the pockets of her red capri pants and joined Jake at the edge of the deck where they couldn't be overheard. "You really didn't think Nina would want Charlie to take the boys anywhere?"

"She's only known the guy two months. I wasn't sure how to handle it. It just seemed better to err on the side of caution. If anything ever happened to Ricky or Ryan..."

"If Charlie really cares about Nina, he'll be glad you're looking out for her and the boys."

"I guess that's one way of seeing it." Jake's shoulder brushed hers as he angled himself toward her, and she felt the excitement of standing so close. His body was hard-muscled and solid. She always felt very feminine standing beside him.

Changing the subject, he asked, "Do you think Barbara's mother is forcing her into giving this baby up for adoption?"

After Tori thought about it, she shook her head. "I don't think she's forcing her. Barbara has a mind of her own. But her mom's lack of support has played a part in it. If she had been willing to take the baby and care for him while Barbara went to college, I don't know if she'd be giving him up."

"You're still worried that she'll change her mind."

Quick tears welled up in Tori's eyes. "I'm praying she doesn't."

Jake's gaze was tender as he looked down on her. Then the tenderness changed, becoming need and longing as they both remembered their last kiss.

Tori told herself she should look away. She should move away. She should distance herself from whatever had started twelve years ago, from whatever was happening now. But it was as if a magnetic field surrounded Jake and drew her into it—drew her into him. It immobilized her, mesmerized her, made the atmosphere around them absolutely hum.

The smell of piñon intertwined with the spice of Jake's aftershave. The sudden fire in his dark eyes took her breath away.

"Tori," he growled low in his throat, as if he was fighting the same kind of forces she was and losing the battle, too.

When his arm went around her, she didn't even think about resisting. As his head bent to hers, she raised her chin, knowing full well she was telling him she wanted his kiss. The warning bells in her head couldn't have been louder. Her own good sense urging her to move away couldn't have been more certain. Yet the primitive drumbeat pounding in her heart, the hungry need in Jake's eyes, the ache deep inside her that had been there as long as she could remember, overshadowed reason and warnings she didn't want to heed.

The moment Jake's lips settled on hers, the earth as she knew it spun. There was no north or south or east or west, only the dizzying height of being at the top of a mountain with Jake. Maybe that was why she wanted his kiss again—because it took her someplace she'd never been. It took her to a peak she'd never climbed. It took her out of herself and into him.

As his tongue breached her lips, her hands went to his shoulders and she held on to him as if he was the center of all the intoxicating sensations whirling inside her. She'd never felt so much a woman. She'd never been with such a virile, sensual man. He tasted her as if he didn't want to miss any bit of her flavor. He swept her mouth as if she were a new world he wanted to conquer. When he slid his hands up into her hair and brought her even closer he let her feel the arousal inflaming them both.

This time when he withdrew he did it slowly and reluctantly. He was breathing hard and it seemed to take him a few seconds to right his world. "We're combustible." He gave a frustrated shake of his head as he dropped his arms to his sides and took a step away so their bodies weren't touching. "But we can't let this play out."

"Jake..."

He shook his head before she could put what she was feeling into words. "I'm not into relationships and commitment and responsibility for someone else's happiness."

His assumption that she expected a kiss to lead to a lifelong commitment made her angry. "And you think I am? I'm not," she stated defiantly. "I know men don't know how to stay. I know they make promises they never intend to keep. I know what it felt like when my father walked out. I know what it felt like when my husband walked out. Do you think I'd ever want to experience that kind of pain again? Do you think I could ever trust a man again?"

After a deep breath, she warned him, "Don't make assumptions about me, Jake. Maybe we *are* combustible. Maybe we have chemistry. Maybe we're both just looking for a distraction because our lives are a little complicated right now. I was a starry-eyed teenager once, but I'm an adult now, and I know there's no place called Camelot."

She stepped away from him before he could back any farther away from her. "I'd better leave. Then neither of us will have to deal with this chemistry that's just too messy to handle."

He caught her arm as she turned. "You're a beautiful woman, Tori. You deserve more than I can offer you."

Pulling out of his grasp, she shook her head. "You've read me all wrong, Jake. I'm not looking for anything a man has to offer. I'm going to have a baby, raise my son and work at making a good life for us both. That's all I want and all I need."

Then, convincing herself that everything she'd just told Jake was the absolute truth, she turned her back on him and went inside.

Jake waited at the local pancake house early the next morning, considering what he was about to do. When Phil Trujillo walked in, the considering stopped and he knew he couldn't let Nina get into a relationship like the one she'd had with Frank. Not if he could help it.

The two men greeted each other, and Phil said, "It was good to hear from you. But you know I can't talk about the burglary case, if that's what's on your mind."

"No, that's not it."

Phil gave him a curious glance as the hostess walked them to a table. After a quick scan of the menus, they placed their orders.

"So how have you been?" Phil asked. "Rumor has it now that you've moved back you might want to look for a job with us."

"Rumor has it wrong."

Phil cocked his head. "Then what's this about?"

"My sister is dating someone. I want to make sure he doesn't have anything in his past she should know about."

"Do you have reason to think he would?" Phil asked.

"No. But she's a widow now, and the man she married had gambling debts she never knew about. She had to use his life insurance to pay off the credit card cash advances, a loan at the bank and the IRS. I don't want her setting foot into another mess."

"I can understand that."

Jake slid a piece of paper across the table. "Here's his name, birth date and car license number."

"That'll do it. She knows or doesn't know you're doing this?"

"Doesn't know. She'll be mad as hell if she finds out."

Phil nodded. "No need for her to find out if this guy's on the level. I'll see what I can come up with." He gave Jake another long look. "Sure you don't want to talk about coming back to police work? What happened in Albuquerque wasn't your fault. You do know that, don't you?"

"That's what people tell me, but I don't believe it."

"So you're going to stay in the handyman business?" Phil's tone was wry.

"I don't know about that, either. A high-school friend of mine just opened a lodge in Crested Butte, Colorado. He wants me to come up, look around and maybe invest as a partner."

"Trading the Sangre de Cristos for the Rockies. Is that something you really want to consider?"

"The truth is, nothing feels right. Until it does, I'm not going to complicate my life even more by making the wrong decision." Ever since Tori Phillips had come back into his life, the wrong decisions were tempting ones. In the past, he'd become involved only with women who didn't want a commitment any more than he did. Although Tori had declared otherwise, she wasn't one of those women.

When the waitress brought their order, Phil smiled and pointed to his chocolate-chip pancakes topped with whipped cream. "Now this is what life should be about."

Jake understood what his friend meant. Unfortunately he rarely took time away from work, from thinking about the past, from wondering about the future, to enjoy a breakfast of chocolate-chip pancakes.

Maybe that would have to change.

Chapter Five

Tori took the day off on Friday and let Loretta and Mary Beth cover for her at the gallery. It was one of the advantages of being the owner. She'd stayed home to sort through the baby things she'd already bought, to see if she'd forgotten anything important. When she finished with the painting next week, she'd have the furniture delivered.

After she washed and folded infant T-shirts and terry playsuits, she hung festively patterned, blue-green curtains in the bathroom. Placing matching rugs on the floor, she not only thought about the baby who would be coming into her life, but Jake. She'd walked away from him in frustration and exasperation on Sunday evening, knowing he was right, wishing their backgrounds had been different. Her reaction to him and to his kisses still caused turmoil she couldn't banish.

From the work he'd done for her, it was easy to see he was a perfectionist. The tile work was absolutely beautiful. Hand-painted white tiles with Native-American designs alternated with blue and green. Floor tiles were a light shade of rust, bordered by blue-green. The medicine cabinet had been hung perfectly, and the light fixture above it was just the right height. All Jake's work showed painstaking attention to detail.

Yet his life was unsettled and his future a question mark. His feelings about relationships and commitment were implacable. Still, his words didn't ring quite true. He *did* know how to commit. He was committed to his family. At least, he was committed to them while he was living in Santa Fe. Maybe, just like Dave and her father, he could be here today and gone tomorrow. Maybe that was what he'd been trying to tell her.

It was late afternoon when Tori heard the clink of her mailbox lid closing. Retrieving the mail from her porch, she brought it inside, riffling through the advertisements and legal-sized letters. She stopped when she came to the one with Jake's return address. Setting the others on the kitchen counter, she opened his and saw it was a bill for the work he'd completed. Just a bill.

Why would he write you a note after the way you left on Sunday night?

When there was a knock at her front door, she opened it to find Barbara, her red Mustang parked at the curb.

"I went to the gallery, but Loretta said you weren't coming in today. I took a chance you'd be here."

As Tori motioned the teenager inside, she assured her, "You can always reach me on my cell phone. You have the number, right?"

"Yes, I have it." Barbara's gaze landed on the pile of baby clothes stacked on the armchair. Quickly, she looked away to the small kiva fireplace, then back at Tori. "I found a natural childbirth class. It's at the Yoga Center next Wednesday night. Are you free?"

"There's nothing on my calendar. But, Barbara, are you sure you want me to be your coach? Maybe your mom would like to help you."

"My mom couldn't care less how I have this baby," Barbara responded morosely. "I've told you that before."

"I'm sure she cares about *you,* though." Tori couldn't imagine having a child in Barbara's situation and not wanting to be with her throughout the ordeal.

Lowering herself onto the sofa, Barbara rested her head against the back cushion and closed her eyes. "My mom has selective vision and hearing. She sees what she wants to see, and she hears what she wants to hear. Nothing else makes an impact."

Opening her eyes again, she sat up straighter. "It's just like this morning. She wanted me to run a whole bunch of errands with her—grocery shopping, picking up dry cleaning, stopping at the jewelry store to pick out something for my aunt's birthday. I told her when I got up that I was tired and didn't feel good. I just wanted to lie low."

"You aren't feeling well?" Tori studied Barbara more closely.

"It wasn't anything to call the doctor about. I felt a bit sick to my stomach, my back hurt and my feet were a little swollen." She peered down at her sandals. "I feel better now. But all Mom could think about this morning was what *she* wanted to do."

"Maybe she just wants to *be* with you, and errands were one way of accomplishing that."

After a pause, Barbara admitted, "Maybe. Almost two more weeks of this. And that's if the baby's on time. I read those books Nina gave me. I could go two weeks *past* my due date." With a sigh, she pushed herself to the edge of the sofa. "I'd better go. I just wanted to talk to you…because I knew you would understand."

Although Tori had always offered Barbara a listening ear, she didn't fully understand. But she was glad the teenager could talk to her. "I'm concerned about you and your baby. You can always reach me."

Barbara's eyes misted a bit, then she pushed herself to her feet. "Mom's going to the opera tonight. Maybe I can help her pick out what she should wear."

"That sounds like fun," Tori said sincerely, remembering the times her own mother had a holiday party at work and she'd helped her decide what outfit looked best.

After Tori walked Barbara outside and waited until she drove away, she felt vaguely unsettled by the visit. Maybe it was the talk about mothers and daughters. Maybe it was Barbara's mother's lack of support for her daughter. Maybe she was worried about Barbara not feeling well this morning. Or maybe she just couldn't keep a tight lid on the fear that not all would go smoothly with the labor, delivery and the adoption itself.

She was still holding Jake's bill in her hand.

I might as well write a check now and take care of it. But as she took her checkbook from one of the kitchen drawers where she kept her bills, she felt an overwhelming urge to see Jake. It was ridiculous.

Or maybe it wasn't. He was a good listener. Besides that, no one from the Santa Fe Police Department had given her any more information about the break-in at the jewelry store. Maybe Jake would know more about that. And if he didn't, maybe he could find out for her.

She checked the return address on the envelope. She was familiar with the area and the apartment complex. She would finish the laundry, give the house a quick dusting and make herself something to eat. Meanwhile, she'd think about delivering the check to Jake in person.

Wavering between her desire to see Jake and the foolhardiness of doing so, Tori didn't actually slide into her car until almost seven-thirty. With the check and her cell phone in her purse, she headed for the Sunset Apartment complex, just off St. Francis Drive. Twenty minutes later she turned into the driveway that led to the parking lot.

The cream-colored stucco buildings were about five years old and well kept. The rock and shrub gardens were relatively low maintenance. Pink concrete paths led to three separate buildings and were lined with garden lanterns that glowed in the dusk. Jake lived in building three.

As Tori started down the walkway, she prepared herself for the possibility that he wouldn't be home. If he wasn't, she'd simply drop the check in the mail and that would be that.

At the building's entrance, she went through a gate that led into a small courtyard. Taking the outside stairway to the second floor, she spotted Jake's truck on the other side of the building. Her heart raced a little faster, and it had nothing to do with climbing the steps.

At Jake's apartment, she quickly pushed the bell. After a few seconds he opened the door, dressed in a black-and-white tank top, black running shorts and athletic shoes. In running gear he seemed even more masculine than usual—more tanned, more imposing, more everything.

"Tori!" he said in surprise. "I was just on my way out for a run."

"Do you run every night?"

"Three or four times a week. It keeps me in shape the way nothing else can."

"I brought your check, but I..." She hesitated. "I wanted to apologize for the way I left the other night."

Backing up, he motioned her inside, apparently deciding this wasn't a conversation he wanted to have in the hall.

While he shut the door, she glanced around the apartment and was surprised by its sparseness. There was a sofa and coffee table, a small TV and a bench press with weights. She didn't see a picture anywhere…or personal mementoes that he'd collected over the years.

"I don't spend much time here," he said when he noticed her looking around. "So I didn't see any need to clutter it up."

"It's definitely not cluttered." She smiled as she spoke.

"If I move to Colorado, I don't want to worry about having to drag everything along."

"Colorado?"

He gestured her to the sofa but didn't sit himself. "I might invest in a ski lodge. I have a friend who bought a place in Crested Butte."

The news that he had someplace specific to consider was a shock. "I see. Do you ski?"

"Cross-country."

"Colorado would be a change."

He nodded. "A change in scenery, a change in lifestyle. I haven't decided for sure yet, but it's an option."

"It's always good to have options," she agreed, not knowing what else to say.

The quiet stillness of night settling in stole through the living room.

"Jake," she began, determined to make peace with him, "I shouldn't have said what I did on Sunday."

His expression remained emotionless. "Why not? It was honest, wasn't it?"

"Yes, but it was an overreaction to our kiss."

"It doesn't matter, Tori."

It did matter. A lot. After the accident, when she learned she couldn't have children, she'd felt less of a woman. Dave had made her feel as if she were no longer complete. Even after she'd recuperated, he no longer reached for her at night. He no longer put his hand on her arm in a gesture of affection. He no longer wanted her. Jake's hungry kisses had made her feel whole again. For some reason she wanted to explain that to him.

"It *does* matter, Jake. When Dave and I were married—"

The cell phone in her purse sounded. She glanced at it, thought about letting the voice mail take the call, but then remembered Barbara's words earlier—*I was tired and didn't feel good.* "I need to take that," she said to Jake.

Giving an understanding nod, he said, "I'll get us a couple of sodas," and went to the kitchen to give her privacy.

Tori slipped the phone out of her purse. "Hello."

"Tori, it's Barbara." The teenager sounded near tears.

"What's wrong?"

"I'm in the house all alone, and my water broke. I think I'm having contractions, and I don't know what to do."

"How far apart are the contractions?" Tori asked, trying to remain calm. The baby would be eleven days early.

"Seven minutes. Dr. Glessner told me at five minutes I should call her. But I'm scared, Tori. What should I do?"

Jake had returned to the room and Tori held her

hand over the phone. ‘‘Barbara’s water broke. She’s having contractions seven minutes apart.’’

‘‘First baby. Seven minutes. Could go on for a while.’’

Tori’s voice shook a little as she said to Barbara, ‘‘I can call an ambulance for you. Or I can pick you up and take you to the hospital. I think we’ll have time. What do you want to do?’’

Barbara took only a moment to think about it. ‘‘Can you come get me? I don’t want to make a scene with an ambulance and all.’’

‘‘I’ll be there in ten minutes. Do you have a bag packed?’’

‘‘Not yet.’’

‘‘If you can, throw a few things together—a nightgown, toothbrush. But if you don’t feel well enough to do it, I’ll do it for you when I get there. Do you want me to try to contact your mom? Page her?’’

‘‘Absolutely not. I’ll write her a note. If she wants to come to the hospital, she can. But I don’t think she will. She wants no part of what’s happening.’’

‘‘Hold tight. I’ll be there as fast as I can.’’

As she disconnected, she noticed her hands were shaking.

Jake must have noticed, too. He set the sodas on the coffee table. ‘‘Are you okay to drive?’’

‘‘I have to be.’’ She started toward the door.

‘‘Tori, if those contractions get closer together, are you going to be able to handle her?’’

‘‘If I can’t, I’ll call the paramedics.’’

Catching her arm, he asked, ‘‘Do you want some help?’’

Ever since she'd met him, she'd known Jake was the noble, chivalrous type. He always put his own wishes aside for someone else. "You don't want to get more involved. I'll—"

"If anything happened to Barbara or to you because I didn't help, I wouldn't be able to live with myself."

She didn't understand the pain she saw in Jake's eyes. But she knew he was telling her the truth, so she was honest with him. "I'd like to have you along. You're more experienced at this than I am. But I think we should take my car, instead of your truck. That way Barbara can stretch out in the back."

With a nod he agreed. "I'll get my wallet and meet you downstairs."

Tori had never been to Barbara's house before. It was in one of the newer developments off Cerrillos Road. Even though darkness had fallen, the address was easy to read under the glow of the porch light. The house was an elegant, two-story adobe with steps along the side leading to a rooftop patio.

After Tori rapped the knocker on the solid wood door, she waited almost a minute, glanced at Jake, then tried the knob. The door opened.

The entranceway led into a large foyer where steps wound to the upstairs hallway.

"Tori? I'm up here." Barbara's voice was hoarse and scared as she called down to the first floor.

Tori rushed up the steps and Jake followed.

Once upstairs he said, "I'll wait out here. Call me if you need me."

Rushing into the room, Tori found Barbara lying atop the pink eyelet spread on a canopied bed. Panic swept through her, but she forced herself to remain calm as she approached the white bed that had a matching dresser, chest and bookshelf desk. On one wall hung a collector's case of Madame Alexander dolls. The laptop computer on the desk made it obvious to Tori that this girl had everything—except the support of her mother.

"They're coming every three minutes," Barbara wailed. "I haven't had a chance to put a suitcase together or get dressed. My suitcase is in the hall closet—"

She gasped and bit her lip. Tori knew another contraction was on its way.

"Jake Galeno drove me here in case I needed help with you."

"I don't want anyone to see me like this." A cry escaped Barbara's lips as the contraction took hold of her.

"Jake was a coach, remember? He might be able to help you breathe through this better than I can."

Tears welled up in Barbara's eyes at the pain ripping through her. Between clenched teeth she mumbled, "All right. Get him."

Instead of leaving Barbara, Tori kept hold of the girl's hand. "Jake!"

The next moment he was beside her.

"Can you tell her how to breathe?" Tori asked him. "It might help. She says the contractions are coming three minutes apart."

"Three minutes? We need to get her to the hospital. Barbara, I want you to listen to me."

His tone was even and calm and seemed to soothe

Tori, too. ‘‘In between the contractions, take normal, natural breaths.’’ He saw she was wearing a sapphire ring on her left hand. Taking her hand, he pointed to the ring. ‘‘When the contraction begins, I want you to focus on this. Look at the stone and breathe in through your nose and out your mouth until the contraction ends. I’ll be driving, but Tori will be with you in the back seat. She’ll help you concentrate on your breathing. That will help the pain.’’

‘‘It’s like my body isn’t even my own! I hate this. I just want it to be over.’’

‘‘Then let us get you to the hospital. I’m going to carry you down the steps and take you to the car.’’

‘‘But my things…’’

Tori saw Barbara’s nightgown and robe hanging on a hook on the dressing room door. She grabbed those. ‘‘Your mom can bring you anything else you need when she comes to see you.’’

‘‘She won’t come.’’

Tori looked Barbara squarely in the eye. ‘‘Your mother cares about you. Certainly she’ll bring anything you need to the hospital.’’

Another contraction overtook Barbara. Jake reminded her about staring at the ring and about taking even, rhythmic breaths. She did that and didn’t seem as scared this time as the pain grabbed her and then ebbed away.

Gathering her up into his arms, Jake was almost to the door when Barbara pointed to her desk. ‘‘There’s a note for my mom. Would you put it on the refrigerator downstairs, Tori, so she sees it? And I need my purse. It has my insurance card in it.’’

Amazed by Barbara's sense of responsibility at a time like this, Tori picked up the note and lifted the leather purse from the desk as Jake carried the teenager out of the room.

A few minutes later, Tori opened the back door of her sedan. Jake propped Barbara by the car as they waited for another contraction to pass. When Tori slid in beside Barbara and timed the contractions, many thoughts flew through her head. Uppermost was the way Jake had handled the teenager. He was so dependable, so solid, so confident. If he hadn't come with her tonight, she would have had to call the paramedics. She would have felt so alone.

When Jake started the car, she curved her arm around Barbara. "We'll be there in no time. We're going to make it."

"I don't know how much more of this I can take," Barbara moaned.

Seeing Barbara in labor reminded Tori she would never experience this life-changing process. If only Barbara could understand how important every step of this was. If only she could realize that an absolute miracle was occurring, she might never put this baby up for adoption.

The lights were with Jake and he pulled up in front of the emergency room at St. Vincent Hospital less than ten minutes later. The tan adobe edifice sat at the foot of the mountains. It was a tranquil scene in daylight. Now, in the dark, with Barbara breathing through contractions, all Tori felt was nervous.

The terra-cotta-and-teal waiting room was more welcoming than hospital lounges in most big cities.

Barbara had called her obstetrician who had instructed her to go to the O.B. unit. Jake didn't leave Tori's side, and she was grateful for that. It wasn't only chemistry between them. There was a connection that went back twelve years, and right now that felt comforting.

As Dr. Glessner facilitated the check-in, Barbara insisted she wanted both Tori and Jake with her.

Dr. Glessner looked baffled. "Neither of them are related to you."

"Tori will be adopting my baby. And Jake…he's been coaching me. Please let them stay with me. I think it'll be…easier. Can't you just pretend they're my parents since my mom's not here?"

"Since you're eighteen, this is your choice. We'll get gowns and hats." Turning to Jake and Tori, she said, "Just give us a few moments to get her prepared in a labor-delivery suite. I'll send somebody for you when she's ready."

As a nurse helped Barbara into a wheelchair and pushed her toward the suite, Tori turned to Jake. "I understand if you don't want to be pulled into this."

"I think it's too late," he said with a wry grin. "I remember how scared Nina was before the twins were born."

"You were very good with her. With Barbara, I mean. I would guess you were very good at your job."

He shook his head. "Let's not go there, Tori. I told you I learned how to negotiate with my father. That just carried over into the work I did."

"I have a feeling you've perfected it even more.

Not everyone can stay calm in a crisis. Not just anyone can talk a teenager into concentrating on her ring.''

He shrugged. ''I know you're trying to distract yourself from what's happening. But I'd rather talk about something other than what I used to do.''

As she studied him, she realized Jake had never been one to talk about himself. But now he apparently had good reason for not wanting to. He was right about her needing a distraction. Then a thought hit her. ''I don't have the baby's room ready yet. I don't even have the furniture!''

''I saw all that stuff you shoved in the closet. You can't tell me you're not ready. As far as the furniture goes, Nina might have an old portable crib in her storage shed that you can use until whatever you ordered is delivered.''

''She still has the twins' baby things?''

''Nina is sentimental. I know for sure she has one of those small, collapsible cribs and their christening clothes.''

''I'll need to buy formula and bottles, too. I was going to paint next week....''

A nurse approached just then, and a few minutes later they were dressed in scrub gowns and hats and were ushered into the suite where Barbara lay on a birthing bed.

Tori hurried to her side. ''How are you doing?''

Barbara's face was red and there were tears on her cheeks. ''They're coming faster. They feel like they're ripping me apart. Maybe something's wrong.''

Tori and Jake both looked with concern at the doctor, who smiled knowingly. ''She's fine.'' She motioned to the fetal monitor. ‘‘The baby’s fine. Just a little while now.’’

When Barbara let out a cry, Jake took her hand, putting the ring in her eyesight. In a tranquil voice he murmured, ‘‘One, two, three, breathe. One, two, three, breathe.’’

The doctor spoke to Barbara steadily. ‘‘During the next contraction, I want you to push. Push with all your might. Are you ready?’’

Barbara glanced from Tori to Jake, and then back at the doctor and nodded. ‘‘I just want this finished,’’ she said. ‘‘I want my life back.’’

Though Tori knew that when women were in the throes of labor pain, they often said things they didn’t mean, she realized in this case, Barbara’s heartfelt statement rang true.

During the next two contractions, Tori found herself breathing along with Barbara. Her gaze locked with Jake’s, and his eyes were as intense as the feelings swirling inside of her.

Finally the doctor alerted them. ‘‘I see the head. Come on, Barbara. Let’s do it this time. He’s ready to come out.’’

Barbara weakly shook her head. ‘‘I can’t do it another time.’’

Tori stroked the girl’s matted and damp hair. ‘‘Yes, you can. Come on, one last push.’’ She felt like an older sister to this girl.

Taking encouragement from Tori, Barbara’s face reddened with exertion as she pushed with all her might.

With a wide smile, the doctor announced, "You did it, Barbara! He's here."

A sweet exultation gripped Tori's heart as her gaze fixed on the baby boy in the mirror. After quick ministrations by a nurse, he was in Barbara's arms, and the teenager was looking down at him as any mother would.

Fear washed over Tori. Jake came and stood behind her, and she felt his chest against her back as she waited for Barbara's reaction...for what she would do and what she would say. It would set the course for the future.

With tears running down her cheeks, Barbara held the baby out to Tori. "I guess he's yours now."

Barbara's woeful voice almost tore Tori's heart in two. Then she felt Jake's hand on her shoulder, and she reached for the baby who would become her life.

Chapter Six

As Tori looked down at the little boy she intended to name Andrew, she pushed his dark brown hair over his brow and stared into his very blue eyes.

Do you know you're my son now? she asked silently.

He blinked at her, and she marveled at his perfect little ears, his tiny fingers, his cute snub nose.

Jake leaned over her shoulder and stroked the baby's cheek with a finger. ''He's perfect,'' he murmured.

At that moment Tori knew Jake was feeling the same awe she was.

''What are you going to name him?'' Barbara asked in a small voice.

''Andrew Michael Phillips. What do you think? Does it fit him?'' She wasn't exactly sure how to act with Barbara now. But she didn't want to ignore her or cut her out of the baby's life.

"It sounds like a name for a prince," Barbara said. Then her expression became set. "He's yours now. I don't want to see him again."

"Barbara—"

"I mean it, Tori. I know we have the guardianship papers to sign and all. Tell your lawyer to call mine and we'll do it as soon as we can."

When Andrew started squirming and then let out a wail, the nurse came to take him. "We'll clean him up and diaper him. He'll be in the nursery."

Tori realized there were some things she had to do, too. She touched Barbara's arm. "I'll stop in and see you tomorrow."

"With your lawyer?" Barbara asked.

"With or without my lawyer."

As she and Jake walked out to the hall, Tori felt elated and excited, yet sad, too.

Apparently Jake understood her mixed emotions. "It's bittersweet, isn't it?"

"I feel so sorry for Barbara, yet I want to claim Andrew. I have to let the pediatrician I chose know that he's been born. I have to call my lawyer so we can sign the papers as soon as possible. I want to take Andrew home and let him know I'm his mother."

"He'll know. If Barbara doesn't want to see him again, you can probably talk to the nurses about feeding him yourself. Once the papers are signed and you *are* his legal guardian, you'll have the right."

The right. The right to be Andrew's mother. For sixty days, anyway. If only the roads hadn't been icy that evening. If only Dave had been driving a little more slowly. If only…

With the night's events catching up to her, Tori felt her eyes well with tears.

When she tried to turn away, Jake caught her by the shoulder. "It's okay."

Her tears kept coming, and his arms went around her. She resisted a few moments, and then gave in to the support. He was strength and stability and a harbor—a harbor she needed until she could take a deep breath, square her shoulders and call her lawyer.

A technician rolled an empty gurney down the hall, and Tori leaned away from Jake. "Thank you for everything you did tonight."

"I didn't do anything except chauffeur you to the hospital."

Examining his face, she realized how easily she could fall in love with him. "Does denying your good qualities keep you humble?" she asked lightly.

He dropped his arms and looked uncomfortable. "I'm not denying anything. I do what I have to do, Tori. Just as you do."

"I don't think it's as simple as that. I think you won't admit you're a good man because you're punishing yourself for something."

"I know you have a degree in art history. Did you take a few courses in psychoanalysis, too?"

Hearing the anger under the sarcasm, she suspected she'd hit too near the truth. "Nope. Just a general psych course. But I don't need a textbook or a doctor's shingle to see that you're stuck in some kind of quicksand you can't pull yourself out of."

''Save your imagination for studying Peter Emerson's paintings.''

Her eyes widened at the mention of her newest best-selling artist, and to lessen the tension between them, she let Jake change the subject. ''Did his art impress you?''

''Not any more than he did. You seem to know each other pretty well.''

''We've spent some time together. When I first agreed to take him on, I flew to Phoenix to see his body of work.''

''Is that all you saw?''

The raw desire in Jake's eyes gave Tori a shiver. Could he be jealous? She wasn't the type of woman to falsely feed that jealousy. ''That's all I saw. We spent a lot of time together poring over his paintings. We went to lunch and dinner. But I wasn't in the market for more than an artist to sell and promote in my gallery.''

''And now?''

''When it's not tax season, Peter is deep in his paintings.''

''And you still aren't interested in a serious involvement, anyway,'' Jake said, repeating her words of a few nights ago.

''That's exactly right.'' She looked toward the nursery. ''I want to see Andrew again before I go. Do you mind?''

''No. I don't mind.'' He was wearing the neutral expression again that Tori was beginning to detest. Jake didn't let anyone see what he was feeling or thinking. Had he learned that in his work? When he was younger, he'd been much less guarded.

"Do you think it's too late to call Nina about the crib?" she asked.

Jake shook his head. "On Friday nights she lets the boys stay up later. It's only eleven. They're in bed, but she's probably pulling laundry out of the dryer. Give her a call. If she says you can use the crib, I'll bring it over to your place in the morning. You might need some help putting it together."

Realizing how much of a help Jake had been, he might have gotten the wrong idea. "I hope you don't see me as a helpless female who can't do anything on her own. Because if that's the case..."

Holding up both hands to stop her words, he assured her, "I see you as a friend of my sister's."

Curiosity and the need to get close to him urged her to ask, "Aren't you and I friends, Jake?" There was a challenge in her question, and apparently he heard it.

His lips quirked up in a small smile. "We're getting there."

This crazy dance she and Jake were doing made her feel off balance. His kisses taught her how deep passion could run between a man and a woman. Yet the walls he used to protect his heart seemed impenetrable. Still, having him as a friend made her want to smile.

She headed for the nursery, eager to catch another glimpse of her son.

Jake loaded Nina's crib into the back of his truck. He'd gotten no sleep last night. Every time he'd closed his eyes, he'd seen Tori staring into that nursery, watching her baby boy as if nothing else in the world mattered. The birth of any baby was an awesome thing. But the look on Tori's face as she watched the mirror when Andrew Michael appeared had been a sight Jake would never forget.

He was worried about what would happen to her if this adoption fell through. Then again, Tori Phillips was a strong woman. She wouldn't give up if she truly wanted a baby.

Suddenly he saw the two of them together, in his bed, making their own baby. He swore, blinked the image away and climbed into his truck.

He'd no sooner switched on the ignition when his cell phone rang. Fishing it out of his pocket, he answered, ''Galeno here.''

''Jake. It's Phil. I've got that information you wanted.''

''What did you find out?''

''Charlie Nexley's clean. No record. Pays off his credit card balances every month. I wish *I* could do that. He doesn't even have an outstanding parking ticket. Now, as far as marriages and divorces and that kind of thing, there's nothing for the state of New Mexico. But that leaves forty-nine others.''

''Nina says he's never been married. I'd like to try and make sure about that. I might do some investigating on my own.''

''You know how it's done.''

Phil was hinting that Jake was itching to get back into police work. He wasn't. He was just going to stop at the car dealership where Charlie worked, look at a few cars or trucks and ask a few subtle questions. Nothing complicated. Once he was convinced Charlie was an upstanding guy, he'd drop the whole thing.

"Thanks, Phil, for doing this for me. I owe you."

"You bet you do. I'll remember that."

Jake smiled as he ended the call. He missed guys like Phil. He missed the men and women he'd worked with every day. Before, his work had been filled with people. Now he lived a solitary life—except for his time with Nina and the boys, except when he was around Tori. Around her, he was torn between keeping all his defenses firmly in place or letting them all tumble down. Yet, if they tumbled down, she'd see how raw he was inside. She'd see the turmoil he always strove to hide. She'd see the guilt that woke him in the middle of the night and kept him working with his hands, rather than working with the narcotics squad and being on call for the negotiations team.

He had too much pride to let anyone see all that. He had too much pride to admit he didn't know where his life was going. He thought about Marion's medal tucked away in his wallet and the reason she'd given it to him. Would he ever consider police work again? He doubted it.

When Jake arrived at Tori's house, he spotted a van parked behind her car in the driveway. Peter Emerson? He pushed down disturbing feelings about Peter and Tori together, and went to the back of his truck for the crib. He was hauling it up Tori's front walk when her door opened.

A tall, thin woman who had waist-long hair tied in a ponytail with a colorful pink-and-yellow scarf, stepped onto Tori's porch. She wore black, wire-rimmed spectacles, a tie-died T-shirt in fluorescent pink and green, and blue jeans. Jake estimated she was in her late forties or early fifties.

''Here's your crib now,'' the woman said with a huge smile.

Tori also came outside onto the porch.

''Did you think I'd forget?'' Jake asked seriously.

Tori's cheeks reddened. ''No. But I was afraid I'd miss you. I have to meet my lawyer at the hospital in an hour. We're going to sign the papers.''

Jake could tell she was anxious, but also excited and could hardly contain it. She was wearing a tailored, navy dress with gold buttons and a gold belt. Just looking at her made his temperature go up, and he hated his inability to control his libido around her.

They must have been gazing into each other's eyes for a few moments because the woman cleared her throat.

Blushing again, Tori made the introductions. ''Loretta Murillo, this is Jake Galeno, the friend I told you about who was with me last night when Barbara delivered.'' To Jake she said, ''Loretta's my right hand at the shop. She also insists she's going to baby-sit for me when I need her.''

''I hope that's often. I raised three and they're out on their own now,'' Loretta told Jake. ''I miss not taking care of a little one. I'd better get over to Perceptions or Mary Beth won't be able to get in. And don't you worry about a thing, Tori. She's come a long way since you hired her last spring. The two of us will manage just fine while you get used to being a mom.''

Loretta gave Tori a quick hug, then hurried to her van.

As Jake carried the crib inside, he asked, "You'd let her baby-sit for you?"

"I've worked with Loretta for four years now, and I've seen her with her own children. I think I could trust her with Andrew."

"Do you want this in the baby's room?" Jake asked over his shoulder.

"No. In my bedroom. I want him with me. The furniture's going to be delivered on Tuesday, and I'll get the baby's room ready then."

When Jake passed the nursery, he could see that Tori had hung some decorations on the walls—colorful cloth hangings of clouds and a hot-air balloon with a little girl and boy swinging in the basket. The places he'd patched had dried to a different color than the old plaster, but with furniture in the room they would hardly be noticeable.

As Jake entered Tori's bedroom, the classic femininity of it kicked him in the gut. There was a light, trace scent of the perfume she wore. The cream spread was covered with a scattering of violets and roses, and her curtains matched. The chenille, braided accent rugs carried tones of pink and violet and green. There were lacy scarves on her dresser and chest, and a silky, pale-pink robe hung on a hook on her closet door. He could imagine her in that robe, its soft material clinging to her body…

"Where do you want this?" he asked huskily.

She motioned to the space between the window and

the bed. "Did Nina have a mattress with it? If not, I can pick one up on my way home today."

"There's a mattress," Jake assured her, "but I'll get the crib set up first. My toolbox is in the truck."

And as soon as the crib was set up, he'd be on his way.

While Jake assembled the bed, he couldn't help but notice that Tori seemed filled with nervous energy. She carried tiny clothes from the closet in the baby's room to her dresser, and then took them back again. She stacked disposable diapers by her bedroom chair, but moved them next to the chest. She went into the laundry room and carried a pile of infant playsuits to her bedroom, dropping them on the bed. But she folded them and refolded them, tucked them into a dresser drawer, then removed them.

Finally, when the crib was standing sturdily on its own, Jake blocked her path and held her by the shoulders. "Tori, what are you doing?"

She looked a bit flustered. "I'm...I'm getting things ready."

"No, you're moving baby clothes from one place to another and then back again with no real purpose."

"Until the furniture comes, I need to keep everything in here. I've decided not to paint for a while, not with an infant here. I'm not sure if I should keep the playsuits by the crib, or the diapers, or—"

"It doesn't matter," he said, enunciating each word. "What's really bothering you?"

She went stock-still, her aquamarine eyes grew big, and she paled a bit. "I've never taken care of a baby before. What if I do something wrong?"

"If you feed him and keep him dry and don't drop him, there's not much you can do wrong." Jake's tone was dry and he hoped it would lighten her mood a bit.

"You make it sound as if this is going to be simple!"

"Maybe not simple. You're going to have to learn to get to know this baby, just like you would anyone else. But from the way you held him and looked at him last night, I know it's not going to take you very long to figure out exactly what he needs."

Tension seemed to slide from her body. Her shoulders, not rigid now, were supple under his fingers. "When I held him last night… I can't begin to explain how I felt. I'd do anything for him. Anything."

He didn't think Tori had ever looked more beautiful, more compassionate, more full of life. It was damned hard for him to drop his hands, to move back to the crib, straighten it and give it a last, experimental jiggle. "I'll get the mattress."

When he went outside, he breathed in a much-needed lungful of fresh air.

"What time is your appointment?" he asked when he returned with the mattress a few minutes later.

Tori was prepared with a fitted sheet, and she slipped it on the bedding now, while he held it. "Ten o'clock."

Jake shifted the mattress into the crib. He'd been wondering about something ever since he'd learned about this adoption. "Mind if I ask why you took the adoption route?"

When she turned away from him to pick up a mobile on the bed, she murmured, "It seemed the most practical...with me being single and all."

Nonchalantly, he lifted the mobile's box, glancing at the directions to see how it should be attached. "What about artificial insemination? Lots of women are choosing that now."

"I didn't have anyone to be a donor," she responded quickly.

"There are anonymous donors. They even come with a medical history."

When Tori was silent for a very long time, Jake looked up.

She was straightening the sheet, avoiding his eyes. Then she sat down on the bed with the mobile in her lap. "I can't have children, Jake. I'll never have my own children."

Her news stunned him. Without thinking about the consequences, he sat on the bed next to her, his shoulder touching hers, his thigh lodged against her hip. "Why not?"

"Six years ago I was in an accident, an automobile accident. Rehab took four months."

Instinctively, his arm went around her. "I'm so sorry, Tori. Are there other repercussions now?"

"Not physical ones. I try to keep myself in good shape and do yoga every day. But the idea of not being able to bear a child was hard for me to accept."

Jake could almost hear what Tori wasn't saying. Certainly a man wouldn't leave because of that. "You said the accident was six years ago?"

She nodded. "A year afterward, my husband asked

for a divorce. He wanted children and I couldn't have them. I couldn't have *his* children.''

The angry oath in Jake's mind wouldn't comfort Tori if it was said aloud. His arm tightened a bit. ''If that's the reason he left, you're better off without him.''

She gazed up at Jake with her eyes full of the pain of everything that had happened. ''I told myself that. But it was difficult putting my marriage and my life with Dave behind me to start over.''

''Was he with you in the accident?''

''He was driving.''

This time Jake couldn't keep his thoughts inside. ''The bastard.''

''He wasn't hurt,'' she added quietly. ''The insurance company decided it wasn't his fault. The other car skidded through a red light. But if we hadn't been going so fast, the accident might not have been as serious as it was.''

After a pause, Jake asked, ''Do you blame him?''

''I wish I could say I was bigger than that. At the beginning I did, especially after he asked for the divorce. But then I realized I was only hurting myself if I didn't let go of the resentment, the bitterness. The insurance settlement enabled me to open the gallery, and I'll always be grateful for that.''

The scent of her perfume, the brush of her silky hair against his hand and her beautiful blue-green eyes tempted him to kiss her again…to lay her down on the bed…to fill the immediate present with sensual pleasure they wouldn't soon forget. But Tori had an appointment with her lawyer in half an hour.

Instead of kissing her, he brought her closer, grazed her forehead with his chin and pulled away. "We'd better get that mobile attached if you want to be on time for your appointment."

Her eyes, which had been vulnerable a moment before, now became guarded. Brushing her hair behind her ear, she stood, the mobile with its bear and donkey and tiger swinging from the music box. "This doesn't look too difficult, Jake. Thanks for bringing the crib over. Tell Nina I'll get it back to her as soon as the furniture arrives."

"You might want to keep it in the living room for when you have the baby in there. You could even wheel it into the kitchen."

She looked down at the wheels. "I hadn't thought about that." A vulnerable look came into her eyes again. "Maybe Nina should give me a crash course on motherhood."

"I'm sure she'd be willing. But I'm also pretty certain she'll tell you that you have to learn by experience."

"Isn't that true of most of life?"

"I suppose it is." Experience had always taught him to tread carefully, keep an even keel, not to reveal too much. And after Marion's death, he'd learned his judgment was flawed and so were his instincts. He couldn't rely on them. He could only rely on what he already knew to be true. Keeping his distance was less hazardous than getting close.

Tori checked her watch. "I'd better leave the rest of this until later. I don't want to be late."

"Are you and Barbara using the same lawyer?"

"My lawyer advised against that. She has her own. Since she's eighteen, she has full say over everything she does. From what she told me, her mother was only too glad to hire and pay for a lawyer to have everything finalized."

"But nothing about this will be final."

"Not yet. In sixty days."

"I know Nina won't mind if you want to call her after you bring the baby home."

"Thanks. I'll let her know how everything's going."

"You don't have to see me out. Good luck with all this, Tori."

"Thanks for your help, Jake, with Barbara and all. I really appreciate it."

"No thanks are necessary. I'll check back in a while and see how you're doing."

He knew he shouldn't. Yet he couldn't just break whatever connection he and Tori had, either. Maybe soon he could figure out why.

When he left, Tori was standing at the crib, fiddling with the mobile. She'd started her life over and she knew where she was going.

Now *he* had to find that same kind of direction.

When Tori brought little Andy into her house in his car seat on Sunday, she set him on the living-room sofa and sat beside him. He'd been crying at the hospital, but as soon as she'd put him in the car and started it, he'd fallen asleep. She was filled with joy and such overwhelming love.

She wanted to call Jake.

But she couldn't…wouldn't…shouldn't.

As she touched the baby's cheeks, dreams of the future ran rampant through her head and she wanted to discuss them with Jake. Everything from nursery school to college, soccer versus football, whether she should encourage Andy to play a musical instrument even if he didn't want to. Somehow, she knew Jake would understand her concerns and her dreams. Yet he wanted to keep his distance, and she didn't know how trusting she could be if they ever did get close.

Unable to resist the temptation of holding her son, Tori unfastened the buckle and gathered him up, crooning to him for a few moments. Maybe her mother would understand what she was feeling. Sylvia Phillips had made arrangements to come visit Tori at the end of October. They had planned her trip considering Barbara might deliver the baby late. The best-laid plans…

Smiling down at her seven-pound bundle, Tori scooted to the other end of the sofa and picked up the cordless phone. She'd tried to call her mom last night, but no one had answered. She hadn't wanted to leave a message about something this important. Later last night, she'd decided to wait to tell her mom the good news until she had Andrew snuggled in her arms.

With Andy in her arms, she was hopeful about everything. Barbara had left the hospital late yesterday afternoon. Tori had hugged her goodbye, and the teenager had seemed relieved that everything was over. Tori was more confident now that the adoption would proceed smoothly. After Tori had signed the guardianship papers, she'd fed Andrew for the first time and felt the stirrings of motherhood take hold of her. She'd gone back again last evening and done the same. The nurse had told her she was a natural, and she had relaxed a bit.

Now she dialed her mother and waited. After Sylvia picked up, Tori said, "I'm a mom!"

"Oh, honey, that's wonderful! How much did he weigh?" Sylvia asked with the same excitement Tori felt.

"Seven pounds, two ounces. He's a perfect armful. He's got dark-brown hair and beautiful gray-blue eyes."

"He's early. Was there a problem?"

"No. There's always room for error with due dates, and the doctor said most babies come into the world when *they're* ready. I wish you could see him."

"I wish I could see him, too. I can't wait to officially be his godmother. The next few weeks will pass so fast you won't know what hit you. I wish I could get off work now and visit, but vacations at the firm are planned months ahead. So is the workload. I can't leave them in the lurch."

Her mother had taken classes at her parish church. Tori had one more sacramental preparation session to attend before Andrew could be baptized. She and Barbara had discussed having the baptism at the beginning of November and Barbara had had no objections. "I know you have to stick to your schedule," Tori said to her mother. "I'll take lots of pictures. You won't miss a thing."

Sylvia laughed and then her laugh dwindled away.

''Tori, there's been something I've wanted to ask you.''

Tori caught the anxious note in her mother's tone. ''What?''

''I've...I've been seeing someone. We've been dating about seven months now, and I think it's serious.''

Sylvia Phillips hadn't dated in all the years since Tori's father had left. She'd never wanted to date, never considered putting herself in the position of having a man leave her again.

Tori swallowed hard. ''What's his name?''

''His name is Sean Brady. He's Irish.''

''Where did you meet him?''

''At the grocery store, of all places. He's the manager. I often saw him there when I did my weekly shopping, and eventually we started nodding to each other. Then one week the cashier made a mistake on my bill, and Sean took care of me at the service desk. It was almost closing time and he insisted on walking me to my car since one of the parking-lot lights was out.'' She hurried on. ''After that...we met for coffee and started going to those weekly senior programs the high school offers. Anyway, we started talking more on the phone, seeing each other more often. He's... he's terrific, Tori, and I want you to meet him. Would you mind if I bring him to Santa Fe when I come? We know your house is small. We'd stay in a hotel.''

When Andy raised one tiny fist to his cheek, Tori tried to absorb everything her mother had said. She touched his curled fingers. When Tori was in college, her mother had moved to Kansas to take care of Tori's grandmother before her death and had decided to stay. She and her mom saw each other only three or four times a year when Tori flew to Kansas or her mom traveled to New Mexico. She'd been so looking forward to this visit.

As if her mother had read her thoughts, she said, "Sean told me he won't hang around all the time because he knows I want to spend time with you. He insists he'll see the sights since he's never been to Santa Fe. We'd still have time together, and I can help you with the baby. Sean's good with babies, too. He has five grandkids. What do you think, honey? If you don't want him to come, I'll just tell him we'll do it another time. Maybe you could meet him at Christmas. But I don't know if you'd want to travel with the baby and all."

Tori hadn't thought ahead to Christmas and traveling to Kansas. From the tone of her mom's voice, Tori could tell her mother really wanted to bring Sean Brady along. It surprised Tori to no end, considering her mom's attitude before this. "By becoming serious, do you mean you're considering marrying again?"

There was a long pause until Sylvia responded, "I know I said I never would. But I hadn't met Sean then. He's nothing like your father."

Just like Jake was nothing like Dave.

You don't know that for sure, an inner voice warned Tori.

Focusing on her mother again, Tori knew she couldn't refuse to meet a man who was becoming important in her mom's life. If this Sean Brady could make her mother happy... "It's fine with me if he wants to come along. But instead of a hotel, I know of a few bed-and-breakfasts that are reasonable. Would you be interested in that instead?''

''A bed-and-breakfast would be lovely.''

''I can make reservations for you, but I need to know—one room or two?''

''One room,'' her mother said quietly. ''I hope you're not shocked.''

Tori wasn't sure if she was or wasn't. Before she could reply, Andy began squirming and his mouth opened in a soft baby cry.

''Uh-oh, Mom. I think it's time to feed the baby. I'll check into the bed-and-breakfasts. At the end of October, availability shouldn't be a problem.''

As Andrew's cries became louder, Tori said goodbye and hung up. Then she went into the kitchen to warm one of the bottles she'd prepared that morning. When she put her baby to her shoulder, she remembered again her father leaving with his suitcases...and Dave's empty closet the day after he'd moved out.

Experience told her that men didn't stay.

She warmed a dish of water in the microwave and then set the bottle in it, putting the idea of calling Jake Galeno out of her head.

Chapter Seven

Tori was juggling Andy from shoulder to shoulder, trying to quiet him, when her doorbell pealed on Wednesday evening. She'd had several visitors bearing gifts—her neighbor, Peter, Mary Beth and Loretta. She wasn't sure anyone else knew about Andy and the adoption.

With Andy wailing, she patted his back, went to the door and found Jake.

He was standing there with some kind of folded table, looking nonchalant, casual and very sexy in a blue chambray shirt and black jeans.

Before she could even say ''hi,'' he explained, ''Nina said this is something you had to have. It's a 'bathinette.' I told her you might not have anywhere to put it—''

She raised her voice over Andy's crying. ''He's having a fussy spell. Come on in.''

After Jake stepped inside, he propped the bathinette against the wall and took Andy from her. ''Sometimes a change helps.''

His slow smile made Tori's heart skip a beat.

The sight of Jake holding her son—she already thought of Andy as her son—made her chest tighten. As soon as Jake had taken Andy, the baby's squalls quieted.

Jake was patting the little boy's back like a pro. Tori decided he'd gotten a lot of experience with babies by helping Nina with the twins when they were smaller.

For the past few days, Tori had tried to keep Jake out of her thoughts. Now with him sitting on the couch with her son, she found it impossible to deny that she'd missed him.

But how could she miss him when he wasn't even part of her life? Or was he becoming a part of her life?

To keep her mind off of the feelings swirling around inside of her, she crossed to the bathinette to examine it. ''I'll call Nina to thank her. That plastic tub is so hard to use. This little hammock should work well. Maybe if I give him a bath, he'll fall asleep.''

''Has he been doing any of that?'' Jake asked wryly.

Jake's hair was mussed by the wind. Instead of imagining herself running her fingers through it, she lifted the little hammock and ran her hand over it. ''Actually, he has. But this is his fussy time, from about five until eight. Then he usually sleeps until two in the morning.''

"If you're getting a couple of good chunks of sleep, you're lucky."

"I called the nurse practitioner about his fussing, and she said it's not unusual. I just have to make sure he's fed and dry and then get through the rest."

"Do you want to try to bathe him?" Jake asked. "Sometimes an extra pair of hands helps."

She had the feeling that Jake preferred doing something other than sitting and making small talk…or letting chemistry pulse between them. That chemistry was getting harder and harder to ignore.

When Jake crossed to her, he easily held Andrew against one shoulder. Pointing to the bathinette, he said, "The top's a changing table. It has a hose so you can drain it into a bucket to empty the water after you fill it. Do you want it in his bedroom?"

"It should fit next to his crib."

Jake handed Andy to her and picked up the bathinette. "I'm sure he'd prefer if you get him ready. I'll set it up."

A few moments later Jake had filled the bathinette, and Tori had attached the little hammock that would support Andy's body above the water.

"This is great," she admitted, as she used baby wash and a soft cloth on her son.

When Andy kicked his legs and seemed to like the feel of the water dripping over him, she and Jake both laughed. Then a silent moment of awareness passed between them.

Taking a deep breath, Tori broke the silence. "Do you think Nina intends to have more children?"

"If this thing works out with Charlie, she might."

''Are you and Charlie getting along any better?''

Jake's forehead creased as he seemed to debate with himself. Then he answered, ''I went into the car dealership when he wasn't there and asked a few questions. Phil checked him out for me, too. His background search didn't turn up anything. So now I guess I should just get to know him better and find out what he's really like.''

''You don't think Nina's doing that?''

''I think her marriage to Frank is something she just wants to forget. I don't want her jumping headlong into another one and then have to deal with those repercussions, too.''

Not wanting Andy to get chilled, Tori finished his bath quickly. Jake appeared at her elbow and peered over her shoulder. When she turned with the baby, she was almost in Jake's arms. ''I've got to get him wrapped up,'' she murmured.

As Jake took the towel she'd hung over the side of the crib and laid it on the bed, Tori saw the nerve in his jaw work. She was glad her hands had something to do. She was glad her eyes had someplace to go other than to Jake's. Why was Jake really here? Because their attraction was tugging at him as it was at her?

While she dried Andy, she tried to steady her pulse. ''The bathinette probably would have fit in my trunk. You didn't have to bring it. Nina could have called me.''

''I thought it would be easier for me to lug it in here than for you to juggle the baby and a bathinette.''

Covering Andy with the towel, her gaze did meet Jake's at that. ''Is that really why you're here, Jake?''

''Nina and I were concerned about you.''

''You and Nina?''

He looked uncomfortable for a moment. ''Sure. You yourself admitted that you've never taken care of a baby.''

''Nina called last night and I filled her in on everything I've been doing.''

''She said you sounded tired.''

''I think that's an expected condition of new mothers.''

Finally Jake confessed, ''Bringing the bathinette seemed like a good excuse to check on you.''

Last week Jake had agreed they were becoming friends. Were they becoming more? Did she *want* more?

When the doorbell rang, it startled them both.

Jake checked his watch. ''It's getting late for visitors.''

''*You're* here.''

With an arch of his brows, he asked, ''Do you want me to answer it while you finish getting Andy ready for bed?''

She lifted her son from the crib and grabbed a diaper. ''Yes, thanks.''

Babies needed constant and immediate attention, and Jake seemed to be aware of that. He'd make a wonderful father. Yet he'd told her that would never happen. She knew part of the reason, but was sure there was more. In spite of caution signals going off, she wanted to know the whole story.

When Jake returned to the room, he was carrying a cardboard box. "It was your neighbor. She said this package came this morning and she had to sign for it."

"FedEx must have tried to deliver it when I went to the store earlier."

"So Andy had his first outing."

She smiled. "I found out it was a little hard juggling a baby and groceries. I just bought the minimum to keep me going. Loretta offered to sit with him this weekend so I could stock up."

"You *do* have to get out, Tori."

"I know. But I hate to leave him. I might take him along to church with me on Sunday. If he fusses, I can always duck out."

After a few beats of silence, Jake stepped closer to her. "You know I said I'd like to get to know Charlie better?"

She nodded, putting the diaper into the crib and gently laying Andy on it.

"How about on Friday night you and me and Nina and Charlie go to that club that just opened—the Southwestern Grille?"

She'd heard of it. A live band played every weekend. Would Jake ask her to dance? She remembered too well the feel of his arms around her. "I don't want to leave Andy for a long time."

"Just a couple of hours. We could leave around nine, be back by eleven."

"I don't know..."

"You have a cell phone, don't you?"

"Yes."

"You can call Loretta every half hour. Most likely, he'll sleep the whole time we're gone."

Jake might be right about that. "So is this a date?" she asked with a touch of humor, yet with the need to know.

"No. I mean…" He seemed off balance, which was unusual for Jake Galeno.

"It's okay, Jake. I get it. It's your chance to interview Charlie on a casual basis. I'm just along for window dressing."

He shook his head in chagrin. "I wouldn't ask just anybody."

That made her laugh.

After tucking Andy into a terry sleeper, she looked at the box Jake had brought in. "It's from Mom!"

Andy was starting to squirm now, and he let out a soft cry.

"I'd better feed him before I open the box. Maybe he'll fall asleep."

A short time later, Jake sat on the sofa watching Tori feed her baby boy. She'd put on a CD of instrumental lullabies while she sat by the fireplace in an antique wooden rocker. All her attention was focused on her son.

Jake remembered watching his mother feed Nina, and he'd often seen Nina feeding the twins. But the sight of Tori holding a bottle for her son did something to him. She was dressed in pale-pink knit slacks with a pink-and-white striped top that delineated her breasts and hugged her slim waist. It was easy to see that she already adored Andy. The strength of the sensations rocking Jake as he watched her unnerved him.

Pushing himself up from the sofa, he went over to a drop-leaf table by the window and examined the baby gifts she'd received.

There was a dish painted with Winnie-the-Pooh characters, along with a cup that wouldn't spill, a white blanket with satin edging, a blue snowsuit and an angel night-light. He picked up a music box that looked to be hand-carved and -painted. Children danced in a ring.

"I have to write thank-you notes for those," she said. "I'm not putting them away until I get to it."

He lifted the music box a little higher. "Whoever gave you this knows fine workmanship. It's superbly crafted."

After a creak of the rocker and a moment of hesitation, she finally revealed, "Peter gave it to me."

Jake's eyes went to hers. She'd said it matter-of-factly, as if Peter Emerson was no different than any other friend. But the music box was expensive, and Jake wondered about the sentiment behind the gift. He abruptly set it on the table. "He's still around?"

"For a short while. His show is scheduled for November third. He'll be back and forth a few times before that. I'm letting Loretta handle most of the details. At first he wasn't comfortable with that, but now I think he sees that she's as competent as I am."

"What kind of details are there to handle?"

Tori shifted Andy to her shoulder to burp him, slowly rubbing his back. "The event is catered, so there's the menu to be decided on, the type of wine to be served. He had to choose a style for the brochure and the invitations, new patrons he wanted to add to his mailing list. Then there are the actual paintings themselves—making sure each is framed properly in the style and color he wants, choosing the best positioning for his work in the gallery. Some artists, like Renée Ludwig—she's a sculptor who's having a show at the gallery the week before Thanksgiving—leave all the details up to me. But Peter isn't like Renée. He prefers to be more involved."

At Andy's burp, Tori smiled, settled him once more in the crook of her arm and offered him the bottle again. "I love the gallery work, but this little guy is going to be my main focus."

This time Andy didn't latch on to the nipple quite as vigorously, and his eyes fluttered closed as he sucked.

"Have you heard from Barbara?" Jake asked.

Tori's expression was a mixture of relief and concern. "No, I haven't. I might not until she signs the final papers. I'd like to know how she's doing, but I don't want to intrude, either. If she's truly trying to get her life back to normal, she might not want to be reminded she had a baby."

"Did you meet her mother?"

"She was there when we signed the guardianship papers. In my mind I'd created this picture of a cold, unfeeling woman. But she wasn't like that. She loves her daughter and she wants what's best for her. She's just absolutely sure that isn't raising a child."

For a few moments they both remembered the night Andy was born. Abruptly Jake nodded to the baby. "I think he's out."

Whether or not they wanted it, another bond had

been formed between her and Jake at Andy's birth. "Sometimes I think he's asleep and lay him in his crib. Then a few minutes later he starts crying again. I'll put him in the crib now and we'll see what happens."

Jake followed Tori to her bedroom. When he passed Andy's room, he noticed once more the care with which Tori had decorated it. But apparently Andy was still sleeping in Nina's crib in Tori's room. As he lounged in the doorway, she settled the baby on his back under the mobile and started the music box.

Jake heard her say to Andy, "You're the best little boy in the whole world, and I love you from here to the moon."

Again Jake felt an ache in his chest, a tightening of the emotions that lodged in his throat. Tori was going to be a terrific mother. Jake had no doubt about it.

Out in the hallway she asked, "Would you like something to drink? Wine? Coffee? Soda?"

"Coffee sounds good."

"I made a batch of brownies for the friends who stopped in. Can I tempt you?"

She certainly could. And did. Maybe the brownies could help him concentrate and satisfy one of his *acceptable* appetites. "Brownies sound great."

As Tori put the coffee on, Jake brought her mother's package into the kitchen and set it on the table.

After Tori put two large brownies on a dessert plate, she asked, "How do you take your coffee?"

"Black."

The table in her dining area was round. He sat across from her and watched as she used scissors to cut the tape on the box and then opened it to find a wrapped present with a blue satin bow. She looked like a kid at Christmas. After she carefully slipped off the ribbon, she tore open the paper.

When she lifted the lid, her eyes misted over. "Mom always figures out the perfect gift."

There were two items in the package. Tori took out the first so Jake could see. It was a small silver box. On the top it read *My First Tooth.*

Jake laughed. "Only a mom would think of something like this."

Next Tori lifted out a baby book that had lion cubs, young harp seals, fawns and a parade of ducks playing around the edges of the cover. In the middle was a space for a picture of Andy.

As Tori flipped through the book, she showed Jake a page every now and then. There was a journal page, and on the opposite side, room for pictures of the first smile, the first tooth, the first step.

Following that, she found a section for the christening, as well as the family tree.

Tori sat and stared at that tree for a long while. "I wonder when I should tell him he's adopted."

"That depends on whether Barbara's in his life or not. How are you going to handle that?"

"I'm not sure yet. But I do know I'm always going to tell him the truth. When my father left, I thought I'd done something wrong. I saw Mom crying and I thought I was to blame. I was almost ten when I saw her looking at the newspaper with an odd expression on her face. When I asked what was wrong, she just said that my dad had gotten married again. That's when I asked her what I had done to make him leave. She gave me a big hug and told me it was her fault he left, not mine. I felt as if a huge burden had been lifted.''

''Did you blame your mom for your dad leaving?''

''No. As I got older and he skipped from one woman to the next, I realized *he* was the one with the problem. But I don't think Mom ever accepted that. She always felt she was lacking in some way. But now…'' She stopped.

''Is something different now?''

''She's coming to visit in a few weeks, and she's bringing a man with her. I think she's serious about him.''

''You sound surprised.''

''I am. She's never dated. I think she's always been afraid to love again.''

Like mother like daughter? he wondered, understanding exactly how Tori's background had affected her—the same way his had affected him.

''After your accident did you see specialists about having kids? They can work wonders now.''

''They can't work wonders when nothing's there, Jake. The doctors had to remove my ovaries and uterus. Dave left because there was no hope of ever having a natural child with me.''

The devastation she must have felt about it was well hidden, but still there. He couldn't begin to imagine how a woman would feel if her child-bearing ability was torn away from her…how she must have hated her world, her life, the other driver. No wonder she'd received an insurance settlement large enough to start up a gallery. "I don't know what to say, Tori. I thought there might be some...hope."

She studied him for a few moments, the vulnerability in her eyes changing to guardedness. "There *is* hope. Andy. And if in a couple of years I want more children, I'll adopt again."

She turned the page in the baby book and then said almost defiantly, "Andy is going to be *my* child. I carried him in my heart just as Barbara carried him in her body. He'll never doubt for a moment that I'm his mom, and I'll love him more than anyone else in this world ever will."

He'd heard of new mothers not bonding with their babies. Tori had already bonded with this infant. It was obvious in the way she handled him, talked to him, thought about him.

She glanced at his coffee mug. "Would you like a refill?"

Her voice didn't carry the warmth it had before, and he wondered what had just happened. Maybe she wanted to get a few good hours of sleep while Andy slept. Maybe she didn't understand his visit or his need to check on her any more than he did. Maybe she was asking him if he wanted to stay or leave.

"No refill." He pushed to his feet. Suddenly he knew if he didn't mention Friday night again and firm up plans with her, she wouldn't go to the club with him.

As she walked him into the living room, he asked, "Nine o'clock on Friday all right?"

"I don't know, Jake."

"It's two hours, Tori. It'll do you good. And it'll

help me see Charlie and Nina as a couple, away from the kids and Mom."

"What do you have against him?"

"He's forty and never been married. I want to know the reason for that."

"You're thirty-four and never been married."

"Exactly. I have reasons. I'm sure he does, too. If he doesn't, then maybe he's the love-'em-and-leave-'em type. Nina doesn't need that kind of heartache."

"She's a grown woman."

"She's my sister."

Tori's voice softened. "All right. I'll come along under one condition."

"What's that?" he asked warily.

"I'm going to call home at least every half hour."

"Granted."

"And you have to promise that you'll go to that club with a mind-set of building a friendship with Charlie, not as an interrogator."

"You're tough," he said with a grin.

"You're not the only one who knows how to negotiate."

He could tell she'd used the word on purpose. To see if he commented on it? To see if it bothered him? It wasn't the word that bothered him. It was his poor judgment in thinking Marion had been ready for the kind of negotiation they'd needed that day.

To Tori he said simply, "I'll remember that." In spite of himself, he was looking forward to Friday night.

Jake was repairing the front coyote fence at a work site the following morning when a navy sedan pulled up to the curb. A few moments later a tall, silver-haired man emerged from the car and approached. Jake recognized him instantly. Don Garcia wasn't in uniform now. Still, the chief of police of the Santa Fe Police Department had an authoritative stature in or out of the official duds. For a moment he wondered how the chief knew where to find him. Then he remembered he'd outlined his upcoming work schedule to Phil.

The chief extended his hand. "Good to see you, Galeno. We've met at a few conferences."

Exasperated that Phil had apparently considered his return to Santa Fe food for discussion, Jake shook the chief's hand. "Chief. What can I do for you?"

"I won't interrupt your work for long. But I thought there might be something *I* can do for *you.* Trujillo told me you're at loose ends."

Jake dropped the handsaw against the fence and tamped down his anger. Phil didn't know how to keep his nose where it belonged. "Not exactly at loose ends. Just in a different line of work."

"Running some kind of business doing repairs and laying ceramic tile?" The chief's voice said that was hardly the caliber of the work Jake had been doing before.

"That's right, Chief. I give an honest day's work for an honest day's pay. At the end of the day I load up my truck and go home. There's nothing on my mind except what's for supper."

"Is this going to last long?" the chief asked.

"You mean my business?"

''No. The attitude that you don't care about the world in general.''

Jake was silent.

''I don't know you well, Galeno. We've only met a few times. But I've always been impressed with you. More important, I've been impressed with your record. Have you kept count of how many lives you've saved?''

''I've counted the ones I've lost.''

''I don't doubt that you have. I know what happened in Albuquerque.''

It seemed everyone in law enforcement did. Word carried from one department to the next. ''Then maybe you'll understand why I like to go home at the end of the day with nothing more on my mind than ordering a pizza for supper.''

The chief's mouth twisted into a grimace. ''I don't believe it for a minute. I might not know you, but I know men like you. I've also known men who have been through what you've been through and haven't faced it.''

''With due respect, Chief, I face it every day, every waking moment.''

The man's gray eyes said he had the knowledge of experience. ''You're not facing it. You're reliving it. That won't do you or anyone else any good. Even if you made a mistake, and from the reports I've received I don't believe you did, you won't move past this until you look at what happened, see it for what it was and know you did your best. That's all any of us can do.''

"If my best isn't good enough, then I should stay out of police work."

"If you don't get past this, Galeno, nothing in your life is going to make sense. Believe me. I've seen it happen to too many men. You think you're moving on because you're keeping a roof over your head and food on the table. But as long as you're still waking up in the middle of the night blaming yourself, not one damn thing about your life is going to work any length of time."

"Why did you really stop by?" Jake asked.

"Because I wanted to feel you out and see where your head was. As I said, good men are hard to find. Especially those with your experience."

"I'm happy with what I'm doing."

"If that's really true, that's terrific. But if you ever want more than that, give me a call."

After he handed Jake a business card, he followed the sidewalk to his car and climbed inside. Moments later, he drove away.

Jake stuffed the card into his back jeans pocket and retrieved his saw. He wouldn't be calling the chief. He would make the rest of his life work—*without* a career in law enforcement.

Chapter Eight

When Jake arrived at Tori's house on Friday evening, Loretta let him in. "Tori's giving Andy his bottle. Apparently he's been pretty fussy since around six. He's only settled down in the past half hour or so."

"Maybe she won't want to leave him."

"The best thing for that girl right now is a break. If you've ever been with a crying baby longer than thirty minutes, you know how draining it can be."

Jake remembered one particular weekend when Ryan had had an earache, and he'd rocked the little boy while Nina had gotten some much-needed rest. Taking care of a child was exhausting when everything went as planned, let alone when it didn't.

In the hall, Jake could hear Tori singing softly to the baby. He found her in Andy's room, sitting in a glider rocker. She set the bottle on the small table next to the chair when he walked in.

"Loretta said you had a rough evening. If you don't want to go, I'll understand."

Tori looked down at her son, then back at Jake. He could see she was torn. "Let me put him in his crib and see if he stays asleep," she said. "If he does, an hour or so out of the house might be good for me. Especially if he's fussy again when he wakes up. I can't imagine how Nina handled twins."

"She had Mom. And Frank was home more at the beginning of their marriage."

When Tori lay Andy in his crib, he didn't stir, just made a contented baby noise.

She smiled. "I moved him in here now, knowing that's best for both of us. Yet sometimes in the middle of the night I just lie in bed and listen to him on the baby monitor. It doesn't make any sense when I should be getting sleep, but his little sounds are reassuring. I know he's okay, and everything seems right in the world."

Leaning down, she kissed the baby's forehead and then joined Jake in the doorway.

"So far, so good," he said in a low voice.

"I'll finish getting ready. If he's still sleeping in five to ten minutes, then we'll slip out."

Jake didn't think Tori had anything to finish about getting ready. She was wearing a black dress with a mandarin collar and tiny little buttons that started at the neck and went to the hem at her knees. Her black pumps showed off her legs. He could imagine unfastening those tiny buttons, running his hands over her curves...

''You look ready now,'' he said with a casualness he wasn't feeling.

''I want to run a brush through my hair and put on some lipstick.''

His gaze went to her lips and he thought about nibbling on the fullness of the lower one, about tracing the upper one with his tongue. Why couldn't he keep his thoughts in line whenever he was around Tori?

''I'll wait for you in the living room.'' At least with Charlie and Nina along—they'd be meeting Tori and him at the club—he wouldn't have to worry about saying or doing something that would get them both into trouble.

Fifteen minutes later, Jake pulled into the parking lot of the Southwestern Grille and Dance Club. As he led Tori inside, the aroma of steak and onions was potent, but not as potent as Tori's perfume. He'd turned on the heater in the truck to ward off the evening chill, but her flowery scent had filled the cab, along with the heat. Now as they found a table for four in the restaurant adorned with Western paraphernalia—from sheriff's badges to wanted-outlaw posters to the chaps hanging on the wall near the corner of the table they chose—Tori slipped off her sweater-coat and hung it on the back of her chair.

She didn't wait for him to seat her and smiled at him as he lowered himself across from her. ''I spoke to Father Gerard this morning. He scheduled Andy's christening after mass the weekend Mom's coming.

I'd like you and Nina to be there, too. We'll have a get-together at the house afterward.''

''That sounds nice. Will your mom help you?''

''I hope so. Since she's bringing Mr. Brady, I won't have as much time with her.''

''You're disappointed, aren't you.'' He could tell from the tone of her voice.

''I guess I am. I was thinking she'd be around to talk to during evening feedings, that we'd catch up on things that we haven't had time to talk about. But I'm happy for her, too. I just hope...''

''What?''

''That she doesn't get hurt again.''

''Maybe you'll have a better read on that after you meet the man.''

''Maybe. Has *your* mother dated since your dad died?''

''No way, no how. She's happy with her life. She likes her freedom and not watching what she says. She enjoys taking care of Nina's kids.''

When Tori studied Jake, he almost got lost in the blue-green depths of her eyes. ''You really believe marriage is a trap, don't you?'' she asked.

''I grew up knowing it.''

''What about love?''

He shook his head. ''I don't know, Tori. Maybe I don't believe in it. Maybe I don't believe anyone can care that much about another person to make forever vows, to make sacrifices. It seems men and women are just too selfish to keep lifelong commitments, to care about somebody else as much as they care about themselves.''

Tori seemed to think about what he'd said, then she murmured, ''That's why men leave.''

''It's not only men,'' Jake insisted, trying to keep the edge from his voice.

''I would have stayed in my marriage. My mother would have stayed in hers. And I suspect your mother never would have left, either. It's because of the kids. Now that I have Andy, nothing is more important to me than his welfare. Women just don't decide one day they've had enough and go follow a dream or marry somebody younger.''

''You're generalizing.''

''No. I'm a mother now. And stability is going to be the most important aspect of Andy's life. I'll do everything in my power to make him feel secure.''

''Nina and I probably would have been better off if my mother *had* left.''

''Possibly. But you're viewing what happened with twenty-twenty hindsight. What if she'd been forced to put you in foster care? I'm sure she stayed awake more than one night considering everything.''

Maybe Jake had always looked at his parents' marriage too simplistically. Had his mother believed they'd be torn apart if she left his father?

Before their discussion could go any further, Charlie and Nina walked in, and Jake was relieved.

Then he saw the expression on Charlie's face. Something was brewing, and Jake had a feeling he might know all too well what it was about.

As Nina congratulated Tori again on becoming a mom, she hugged her. Jake could see that Tori was pleased and touched. The two women had evidently tumbled back into a comfortable friendship. His gut told him that Tori could talk to anyone easily and had found her place in social circles he'd never be a part of. Yet she didn't seem to have many close friends. Was trust an issue in all areas of her life? She seemed close to her mother. Maybe she didn't feel she needed anyone else to confide in. Tori was a fascinating mix. So fascinating she was taking up too many of his waking moments, as well as his sleeping ones.

Nina and Tori seemed to have endless things to talk about—Andy, car seats, plans to visit the Georgia O'Keefe Museum together. He tried to make conversation with Charlie, which was what tonight was all about. "Have you ever been here before?" he asked him.

"Once or twice."

"I hear the band playing tonight is supposed to be good."

Charlie shrugged.

As the band took their place on the stage, Jake tried again. "I never could get a handle on line-dancing. What about you?"

Charlie sat up straighter, his shoulders rigid. "I can two-step. That's about all I'll need to do here tonight."

Yep, the man had a burr under his saddle. "I'm just trying to get to know you better, Charlie."

"Well, you're going about it the wrong way."

Hearing the edge in her date's voice, Nina's conversation with Tori stopped in midsentence. She glanced back and forth between the two men. "Is there something going on here I should know?"

"Ask your brother," Charlie instructed her.

''Jake?''

''What's on your mind, Charlie?'' Jake asked, knowing they had to clear the air.

Charlie set his sights on Nina now. ''Did you know he was checking up on me? Did you put him up to it?''

''I don't know what you're talking about.''

Nina was obviously perplexed, and Jake could see Charlie's relief that she was. Nevertheless, the man's anger was still evident as he told her, ''Your brother turned up at the car lot when I wasn't there. He acted like he was looking for a car, but he asked questions about me. Enough questions that my manager asked if I was in some kind of trouble. He thought a PI was on my tail. When I asked for a description of the man asking the questions, I knew it was you.''

''Jake?'' Nina's eyes were filled with hurt and a demand for an explanation.

He wasn't about to apologize for looking out for her. ''I didn't want you to make another mistake. You thought you knew Frank and you didn't. If I had done a background check on *him,* we would have learned that his credit cards were maxed out, that he had loans to repay, and that he had a gambling habit he didn't want to break.''

''Charlie isn't Frank,'' she began, ''and—''

Charlie cut in. ''You did a background check on me?''

The band started playing, and couples began to make their way to the dance floor.

''I didn't do it myself. A friend did it for me.''

''And you asked Charlie's manager questions about him?'' Nina prodded.

Leaning forward, Jake made himself heard over the band's introduction to a country-western classic. ''I wanted to make sure his story was consistent with his background. Frank's gambling left you with a legacy of debt, instead of an insurance policy that could fund part of the boys' education.''

Tori had been quiet, taking in the family tiff, but now she gently touched Nina's arm. ''Jake was just trying to protect you.''

Swinging toward her, Nina shook her head vehemently. ''You might see it as protection. I see it as interference. He has no right to interfere in my life when *his* is a disaster.''

She took Charlie's hand and stood. ''Charlie isn't Frank. And until you decide to accept my decisions and accept the fact that he's going to be part of my life and the boys', you can find somewhere else to go for Sunday dinner.''

Negotiate, Jake's common sense told him. But he was too close to this one, and his pride forced him to say, ''If that's the way you want it.''

His sister looked close to tears, but her pride was as sturdy as his. ''I want you to stop treating me like a baby sister. I'm old enough to know what I want.''

''Years don't always make a difference. Especially when you're trying to grab a dream that got away from you once before.''

Nina shook her head. ''You've lost your hope, Jake. That's what's wrong with your life. I still have mine.''

Charlie curved his arm around Nina's shoulders and

urged her toward the door. ''Come on. I think we'd better have our night on the town somewhere else.''

As the band played their opening number, Nina and Charlie left the club.

Tori's gaze was sympathetic as Jake ran his hand through his hair and leaned back in his chair. ''I sure made a mess of that.''

''Did you really think Charlie wouldn't find out you were the one asking questions?'' Tori asked.

''I didn't care if he did. I thought it would give him a warning that I wouldn't let him take advantage of Nina.''

Tori leaned closer to him so he could hear her above the music. ''It *is* Nina's life.''

He blew out a breath. ''I know that. But ever since she was a kid I've been making sure she doesn't fall out of trees or dive into the deep end alone or play in the street. I've always looked out for her, and I don't see that changing.''

''How are you going to look out for her if you're not invited to Sunday dinner?''

''She won't cut me out of her life.''

''She will if she wants Charlie in her life and you won't accept him. Don't underestimate the bond a man and woman can have when they think they belong together.''

Music played for a few beats. ''Did you and your husband have that kind of bond?'' Jake asked. The information was suddenly very important to him.

''I thought we did before the accident. But since Dave left, maybe we never really had it. Maybe I just wanted it so badly I thought we did.''

The notes coming from the guitars and piano twined into a slow ballad. Jake decided they needed a break from the tension still in the air, as well as this conversation. ''Do you want to check on Andy?''

Tori glanced at her watch. ''If I call too soon, Loretta will think I don't trust her.''

''She knows you're going to be anxious about leaving him. I don't think she'll mind.''

After Tori went to the foyer to make the call, she returned with a smile on her face. ''He's still sleeping. I guess he got all of his fussing out of his system while I was there.''

Before Tori seated herself again, Jake stood. The band drifted into a second slow song. ''Would you like to dance?''

Her hesitation was slight, but he caught it. Still, she said, ''Sure. That would be nice.''

As they walked to the dance floor, Jake realized he didn't give a damn about dancing with Tori; he just wanted to hold her in his arms. How long had it been since he'd held a woman that way? How long had it been since his job had dominated his life? Directed the course of it? Left room for nothing else?

Now he had the room, but he and Tori wanted different things. She was all about permanence and stability and raising her son. He just wanted to slake some of the need he felt whenever he was with her. He wanted to feel alive again.

Tori felt fragile in his arms as they began to dance. He'd taken her right hand and engulfed it in his. She seemed to be keeping a polite space between them, and for now, that was okay. As his gaze met hers, he felt adrenaline rush to every important body part. He brought her a little closer and saw a flush steal into her cheeks. The pulse at her throat beat faster, and her eyes took on a shimmering quality that spoke of a woman's deepest secrets and desires.

Her hand tightened on his shoulder. "Jake, maybe this isn't such a good idea."

He tried to keep the atmosphere light. "I don't have a better one right now." When he passed his hand down her back, he felt her tremble. "Don't we deserve a little pleasure?"

"Is that what you want?"

"I want to concentrate on the moment. Not on what happened yesterday or what might happen tomorrow." Folding their hands into his chest, he murmured, "Relax and just enjoy it."

Following his own instructions, Jake gave himself up to the scent of Tori's perfume, to the sweet temptation of her hair so close to his jaw, to the pleasure of the warmth of her body as his heart beat faster and so did hers. When she didn't pull away or resist, he guessed she'd given herself over to the rhythm of the music and the sweet emotion of the lyrics. However, the desire that danced between them sought a broader stage to perform. He was holding on tightly to the hunger and need and want. If he turned them loose, there'd be hell to pay. He knew that and she did, too. Yet giving primitive needs a little satisfaction tonight seemed like an excellent idea.

When the rhythm of the music overtook them, when Tori pressed tightly against him and he knew she could feel his arousal, kissing her seemed like an even better idea.

In fact, kissing her was necessary.

When the side of his chin brushed her temple, she looked up. He saw a depth of passion in her eyes that he'd always known was there. Years ago, she'd been too young for him to take advantage of it. Now...

When he bent his head, her gaze didn't waver. She knew what was coming and welcomed it. He remembered their other kisses and prepared himself for the rush he knew would propel his desire. As his lips hovered tantalizingly close to hers, he taunted them both with anticipation of it. She lifted her chin higher, and he smiled as his mouth found hers. Tori's response wasn't hesitant tonight. When his tongue slid into her mouth, she accepted him, met him stroke for stroke, played and aroused. His groan vibrated through them both.

As her arms went around his neck, Jake was oblivious to the other couples on the dance floor, to the band, to the lights, to the reasons he should pull away, take her home and leave this life in Santa Fe for something different in Crested Butte.

Suddenly there was applause all around them. Jake loosened his grip on Tori, lifted his head and heard the leader of the band say, "For the couple who hasn't come up for air for at least five minutes."

There were more cheers and applause, and Jake felt himself flush. Apparently everyone else had stopped dancing. He and Tori had still been swaying to the music and kissing at the same time. As Jake protectively kept his arm around Tori, he saw that her cheeks were red, too.

With all the aplomb he could muster, he smiled, raised one hand in a wave and guided Tori back to their table.

Once there he asked, "How about we go back to your place?" He'd take her to his apartment, but he knew she'd never agree to that with her concern about leaving Andy.

Obviously trying to compose herself after the spectacle they'd made of themselves, she avoided his gaze and checked her watch. "That's a good idea. I'll call Loretta and tell her we're heading home."

Home. Even his apartment in Albuquerque hadn't been a home. As a member of the negotiations team, he'd always been on call, worked odd hours and slept on a cot at the station some of the time. Nina's house was a home, but it wasn't his. Now she might not invite him into it again any time soon.

He lifted Tori's sweater from the back of her chair and held it for her. As she slid her arms into the sleeves, he bent close and murmured, "If Andy's still asleep, we could try a second dance at your place."

Although she took a deep breath, she faced him. "I'd like that."

He wondered if she meant she'd like to dance with him again, or she'd like to dance and kiss and see where it led. In less than fifteen minutes he'd find out.

As soon as Tori was home, she checked on Andy, rested her hand on his fine hair and kissed him. Jake had followed her to the doorway of the baby's bedroom, but he didn't step inside.

''How much longer do you think he'll sleep?'' Jake asked.

''I don't know. His schedule changes day by day. The nurse practitioner told me that's normal. Especially in the first couple of weeks.''

When they returned to the living room, Loretta motioned to the kitchen. ''I made a pot of coffee if you're interested.'' She smiled at Tori. ''But I don't call this baby-sitting. Not when he sleeps the whole time I'm here.'' She glanced at the message pad by the phone. ''Right after you called me, Barbara Simmons phoned.''

Tori's expression changed from one of contentment to concern. ''Did she want me to call her back?''

''No. She didn't want the phone to disturb her mother. She said she'd try to get hold of you again tomorrow.''

''Nothing else?''

''I don't know if I'm reading something into it, but she sounded upset.''

''She didn't give any indication why?''

Loretta shook her head. ''No. I'm sorry. I didn't feel it was my place to push her. But you can call her in the morning.''

Tori bit her lower lip and glanced toward Andy's room.

After Loretta left, Jake realized the intimate mood between them had definitely been lost.

In spite of that, Tori asked, ''Would you like that cup of coffee?''

''Rather than a dance?''

''Jake...''

''I know. You're concerned about Barbara calling so late. I guess it won't do any good for me to tell you that worrying all night and losing sleep over that phone call aren't going to help.''

''I've already told myself that,'' she said with a small smile.

She looked vulnerable and alone. If he took her into his arms, he could kiss her to make it better. But her world might tilt a little more, and she didn't need that. ''Thanks for going along tonight.''

''What are you going to do about Nina?''

''I'm going to let her cool off. This isn't the first fight we've had about my big-brother protective streak. I can't apologize for what I did, because I'd do it again.''

''Charlie was angry, too,'' she reminded him.

''Yeah. I might have to do something about him first.''

Then, because Tori looked so beautiful, because his blood was still thrumming from holding her and kissing her, because he didn't know when he was going to see her again, he pulled her into his arms, crushed her lips with his and gave her a thoroughly passionate kiss.

When he stepped away and headed toward the door, he called over his shoulder, ''Think about that, instead of worrying about Barbara's phone call.''

The next morning, when Jake stopped at the car lot where Charlie worked, he saw Nexley's SUV parked by the service garage. The showroom had just opened and Jake spotted the manager standing inside, looking out.

As he opened the heavy glass door, the man's smile disappeared.

''I'm here to see Charlie Nexley,'' Jake said.

The manager pointed down the row of office cubicles. ''Third one.''

Jake strode toward Charlie's office, and he found the man seated at his desk with a stack of papers in front of him. As Jake stepped inside, he closed the door behind him.

Charlie stood, his hands balled into fists. ''What do you want, Galeno?''

''I just want to talk.''

''There's nothing to talk about. You don't think I'm right for your sister—''

''That's not what I think.''

Charlie stopped and cocked his head. ''You sure made it seem that way.''

''I don't know you. I don't know if you're right for Nina or you're not. I just want to make sure you're not *wrong* for her. Has she talked to you about Frank?''

Charlie's stance became a little less defensive. ''She's said a few things. She thought he'd cheated on her when he was traveling.''

He and Nina had never discussed that. The fact that she'd confided her suspicions to Charlie meant she truly did trust him. ''What about the gambling?''

''You mentioned that the other night. Nina didn't want to talk about it afterward. Said her first marriage was finished and she'd moved on.''

"She has. But she hasn't forgotten how much hot water he got them into. Frank was a gambler and a spender. If I had done a background check on him, it would have saved Nina heartache and sleepless nights. He seemed great on the surface. He charmed her when they met and while they were engaged. No one suspected the problems he had or the way he was going to use her."

"I'm not Frank."

"How am I supposed to know that?"

"I guess you're just going to have to give me a chance."

Silence fell between them.

"I don't know how much longer I'm going to be in Santa Fe," Jake finally said. "That's another reason I wanted to check you out."

Charlie appeared to think about that, then he nodded. "All right. You've done that. Let's say I understand why you did it. I have a sister. She's older, but I still feel protective about her, too. She wouldn't like me saying it, but it's true. I care about Nina and Ricky and Ryan. If you're around us much, you'll see that. If you aren't around, you'll just have to trust Nina's judgment."

Jake knew Charlie was right. So he offered an olive branch. "Maybe you and I could take the boys to the park tomorrow. What do you think?"

Charlie's eyes narrowed. "I think you're going to put me through the wringer until you leave Santa Fe. But if that's what it takes for you to trust me with Nina, then give it a try."

That was a challenge, one that Jake was going to take on.

Chapter Nine

On Friday night three weeks later, Tori was still thinking about what might have happened if Jake had stayed when they'd left the Southwestern Grille and gone to her house. She'd as much as sent him away, and she'd convinced herself that had been for the best. Her attention had to be focused on Andy now. He'd been a relatively contented baby when she'd brought him home from the hospital, but his fussing had increased over the past few weeks. When she called the pediatrician, he suggested drops she could buy over the counter at the drugstore. But since last night, they hadn't eased Andy's discomfort, and he was spitting up now and then.

Because he was only a month old, all of it could be attributed to colic or to his digestive system still developing. Yet she felt as if she'd been thrust into the middle of the desert with no shelter or water within sight. As the adage went, babies didn't come with an instruction manual. Tori felt out of her depth, and by Friday night she called Nina.

"How's it going?" her friend asked.

"I think I'm doing something wrong. He's fussy most of the time. Not at all like the first two weeks."

"What does your doctor say?"

"We've changed his formula twice. I had him in last week and I have another appointment on Monday. But something just seems different."

"Different in what way?"

"He's not happy. He doesn't seem satisfied. He's spitting up more than before."

"You can always take him to the ER."

"I'm supposed to call his doctor first. Dr. Johansen is always patient, and he usually returns my call within fifteen minutes. He probably thinks I'm a mother with nothing better to do than worry about her baby."

"That's what mothers do," Nina assured her. "I remember Ricky had a problem with formula. Even after we made the switch, it took a week or so until he adjusted."

"You didn't breast-feed?"

"Are you kidding? With two of them?" Nina laughed. "I wouldn't have had time to brush my hair."

That made Tori smile. "I can't imagine having two crying babies. I just feel so helpless when I can't make him happy."

"So you're one of those," Nina drawled.

"One of what?"

"One of those women who wants everyone in the world to be happy."

"Not everyone in the world. Just my son."

"How many more days until the adoption is final?"

"Thirty-three."

"Have you heard from Barbara?"

"She's been away. She left a message Saturday night when we went to the Southwestern Grille. When I tried to call back, I reached her mother. Mrs. Simmons told me Barbara took a vacation with a friend of hers. They flew to Phoenix. When I called again a few days ago, she still wasn't home."

"What do you think that's all about?"

"I don't know. Barbara said she just wanted her old life back. I guess this is a start."

With the cordless phone at her ear, Tori peeked into Andy's bedroom and could see he was still napping. She breathed a sigh of relief. "Speaking about getting things back to the way they used to be, have you and Jake mended your fences?"

"Charlie and Jake had a talk. They took the boys to the park together the past couple of weekends. Jake and I are being civil, but I'm still a little peeved. He has to stop treating me as if I'm a child."

"You're always going to be his little sister. He was just trying to—"

Nina cut in. "You're becoming his advocate. Does that mean something?"

"I like your brother, and I admire him."

"You *like* Jake?"

Confiding in someone didn't come easy for Tori. If she examined her feelings for Jake too closely, she'd have to admit that *like* didn't begin to cover it. ''I've got my hands full with Andy.''

''Haven't you seen how good Jake is with babies?''

''Nina...'' It was a warning that she wanted this part of the conversation to end.

''Okay. I'll drop it for now. I'd better run. The boys have been quiet for too long. That always spells trouble.''

''Thanks for listening.''

''I'm afraid that's about all I can do. But I will tell you this. Follow your instincts, Tori, where Andy is concerned. You know him. If something doesn't seem right, call the doctor again.''

Over the next twenty-four hours Tori became more and more worried. Andy's fussing lasted for hours. He couldn't keep anything down. By Sunday afternoon she called the pediatrician's service, not caring if they thought she was a bother. Something was wrong.

Dr. Johansen returned Tori's call. He was as concerned as she was. ''Bring him to the emergency room. I'll meet you there.''

Tori was placing Andy in his car seat on the sofa and adjusting the straps when she heard footsteps on her porch and recognized them.

Taking Andy with her, she opened the door. ''Nina told me you were having problems with Andy,'' Jake said. ''Is he any better?'' Worry creased his brow.

In spite of the situation, Tori realized it was Sunday, and Jake must have joined his family for dinner. ''I'm on my way to the ER. Something's wrong, Jake, I know it.''

''I'll follow you there.''

"You don't have to—"

"I saw this baby come into the world, Tori. I feel I'm vested in what happens to him."

"If the doctor admits him, this could take a while."

"It's Sunday. My time's my own."

Tori realized she was beginning to depend on Jake. Didn't she know better than to depend on a man? Yet, right now she wanted him to come along.

As Jake carried Andy in his car seat to her car, she picked up the diaper bag and hurried after him.

After the initial paperwork at registration, a nurse showed them to a centralized intake area with several exam tables. Andy was the only patient at the moment. He was wailing, and Tori tried everything she could think of to comfort him, from hoisting him to her shoulder to offering him a pacifier to rocking and walking him around. Jake tried, too, but nothing helped.

Finally the doctor appeared. Noticing Jake, he cast a questioning look at Tori.

Jake moved forward and extended his hand. "Jake Galeno. I'm a friend."

After a nod, Dr. Johansen began examining Andy. Eventually, he pulled the stethoscope from his ears and addressed Tori. "I'm going to order an ultrasound and consult with a gastroenterologist."

"I want to stay with him."

The older doctor's eyes were kind. "You can do that." The doctor glanced from Tori to Jake. "Mr. Galeno can wait in the lounge. I know you're the baby's legal guardian now, Tori, but you might want to consider notifying his mother. It's your call."

''Do you think this is serious?''

''I won't know until we do the test.''

Tori thought about it. ''Barbara's out of town right now, and I don't know how to get in touch with her. Let's see what the ultrasound shows first.''

After the doctor told Tori he'd meet her in the Radiology Department, she picked up Andy and held him in the crook of her arm. Bending her head, she rubbed her cheek against his. He was quiet for the moment, exhausted from all the crying. His little whimpers tightened her chest.

Crossing to her, Jake clasped her shoulder. ''He's going to be all right.''

''He's so little for tests. He won't understand what they're doing to him.''

''These are professionals, Tori. And you'll be there with him. He'll know that.''

''I'm scared, Jake. Something is seriously wrong.''

His calm voice soothed her. ''Then we'll find out what and fix it.''

An hour later Jake paced the lounge, ready to search out Tori and find out what was going on. Usually he was a patient man. Usually he kept on an even keel, knowing how important that was in making any decision and handling any situation. But today…

He'd stayed away from Tori the past few weeks, hoping distance would quiet his yearning for her, his curiosity about how she was handling motherhood, his need to do more than kiss her. He'd wondered about Barbara's phone call but figured Tori would call Nina if there was a problem. Earlier today when he'd gone to Nina's for dinner, he'd learned Tori had called his sister on Friday worried about Andy's stomach upset. In turn, Jake had worried about them both. He'd had a tight feeling in his gut ever since his life had crossed with Tori's again. Ever since the night Andy had been born, he couldn't seem to disconnect himself from her and the baby she wanted to mother so badly.

When Tori hurried into the lounge, he knew the news wasn't good. Her pretty face was drawn, her posture rigid.

"What is it?"

He watched as she swallowed hard and took a deep breath. "It's a condition called pyloric stenosis. It's a closing of the valve leading to the small intestine. Essentially, it's grown shut and they have to reopen it."

"How did it happen?"

"They don't know how…or why. Apparently, it's more common in first-born males. He'll have an incision above his navel…"

Her voice broke and Jake could see how hard this was for her. She was scared, and he didn't blame her. If he'd been speaking to the doctor, he'd have asked about odds and risks. But now he waited for Tori to tell him anything more that she knew.

"He'll be able to go home the day after tomorrow if everything goes well and he starts eating again. If he doesn't…" Her voice trailed off. Turning away from Jake, she crossed to a painting on the wall and stared at it unseeingly.

Approaching her, he stood behind her, reining in the urge to touch her, reining in so many urges where she was concerned. ''You have to believe the surgery will be successful.''

''I'm trying to believe that. I think it'll help if I go up to the chapel. They wouldn't let me stay with him. They wouldn't let me keep holding him.''

The suggestion the doctor had made about calling Barbara needed to be confronted. Jake didn't want to add turmoil to Tori's life now, but he knew she had to face all the possibilities. ''Are you going to call Barbara?''

''I can try. But I don't know if her mother will give me her number.''

''Calling her will give you something to do while Andy's in surgery.''

''The doctor said it would take about an hour.'' Facing Jake now, she lifted her chin and her gaze collided with his. It was a shock in a way, because he felt so much when he looked into her eyes.

''You don't have to stay,'' she murmured. ''I know you probably have tons of things to do.''

''Yeah, tons,'' he said wryly. ''Believe me, I can fix Ryan's scooter and roughhouse with Ricky just as well another day. Charlie was at Nina's. He'll take up the slack. I think the important question is—do you want me to stay or do you want me to go?''

Jake had always prided himself on being good at reading body language. As Tori brushed her hair behind one ear and shoved her hands into her jeans pockets, he could see she was fighting a battle. He suspected that she wanted to stand on her own two feet, that she didn't want to need anyone. But her innate honesty brought a sad smile to her lips. ''If you want to stay, I'd appreciate the moral support. But I'll understand if the waiting gets old and you want to leave. Sitting around a hospital is never any fun.''

Motioning to the phone, he suggested gently, ''See if you can get Barbara's number. After you call, we'll go up to the chapel together and wait.''

Jake walked to the other side of the lounge to give Tori privacy. A few minutes later, after she hung up the phone, it was easy to read the anger on her face.

''Mrs. Simmons wouldn't give the number to you,'' he guessed.

''No, she wouldn't. I don't understand that woman. Doesn't she think that her daughter has feelings? And that if she doesn't deal with them now, giving up this baby will haunt her for the rest of her life? She said that Barbara needed to make a clean break of it. Mrs. Simmons doesn't want her daughter's vacation ruined.''

Shaking her head in frustration, Tori left the lounge and headed for the elevator.

Jake reached it the same time she did and jabbed the button. ''You realize if Barbara knows about this, you could awaken her motherly instincts.''

When the elevator door swished open, Tori stepped inside and didn't say anything for a few moments. ''I know. But it's the right thing to do, Jake.''

He knew it was, too. Maybe he and Tori were attracted to each other because they believed in doing the right thing. Still, the right thing often caused heartache, took courage and wasn't as easy as making a phone call. Thinking about doing the right thing always led him back to thoughts of Marion and what had happened.

As the elevator slid up a floor, he remembered Marion's funeral. He'd wanted to face her widowed mother after her daughter had died, but his guilt and advice from the police department had kept him from doing that. Now he wished he had. Jake had been trained to follow orders, and he'd stayed away from Elaine Montgomery. But he didn't know now if that had been the right thing to do.

After he opened the door of the chapel for Tori and they stepped inside, he realized why she wanted to come here. The quiet. It was a world away from the hospital bustle, although activity was practically right outside the door.

They walked to the front of the chapel, where a rough-hewn cross hung, as well as a Star of David. When they took seats in the third pew, Jake glanced at the wall beside them, noticing the framed portrait of Nuestra Señora De Los Dolores, Our Lady of Sorrows. Then the dark wood of the altar drew his gaze. A few moments later when he glanced at Tori, she was looking down at her hands and a tear was running slowly down her cheek.

Without a moment's hesitation, he slid closer to her and wrapped an arm around her. Even with his vast experience with words—the calm make-a-deal tone, the believe-and-you-can-trust-me phrases, the coaxing supplications, the firm stand-his-ground negotiation—there were no words for a situation like this. Tori was worried she'd lose her son. He wouldn't serve up platitudes that might not be honest.

When Tori's shoulders relaxed and she leaned against him, he knew she'd finally accepted his support. That seemed to be very important to him, and he didn't examine the reasons too closely.

They sat together like that until the doctor found them. He was smiling, and Jake let out a breath of relief.

Dr. Johansen assured them, "Andy came through the surgery just fine. He's in recovery."

Tori was on her feet immediately. "When can I see him?"

"In about an hour. Why don't you go down to the cafeteria and get yourself something to eat?"

She brushed the notion of food away. "Can I stay tonight? I'll sleep in the lounge."

"I don't think that'll be necessary. We'll roll a recliner next to the crib."

"Are you sure you want to stay, Tori?" Jake asked. "You won't get much sleep. Andy's in good hands—"

"Would you leave if he was *your* son?"

Even if Tori left, Jake had planned to stay. He had a stake in this baby. "No, I wouldn't."

As she studied him, he felt she was seeing too much. Finally she suggested, "Let's go to the cafeteria. I could use a cup of coffee."

Tori didn't say much as they drank cups of black coffee, took a walk through the gift shop, then found their way to Pediatrics. They stood by Andy's crib, watching the nurse attend to him. There were three other children in the unit, one about three years old and two about eight or nine. Their parents were entertaining them.

Finally the nurse left Andy's crib, and Tori said to Jake, "Go home."

"I told you I'd stay."

"I know. And I appreciate it. But it's silly for both of us to lose a night's sleep. Since he's sleeping, I'm going to try and catch a few winks, too." She gestured to the recliner near the foot of the crib.

Although Jake wanted to stay, he really had no place here. Andy was Tori's responsibility, and she seemed to want to handle the burden on her own. She was telling him she didn't need him. "You should eat something before you try to get forty winks."

"I'm not hungry."

"You can't take care of Andy if you don't take care of yourself."

"I promise I'll have a big breakfast in the morning."

Obviously she didn't want his advice. "Will you call me and let me know how Andy's doing? Nina will want to know, too."

"I'll call."

"I have a cell phone, Tori." He pulled out his wallet, took out a business card and handed it to her. "It's the second number. I'll make sure it's turned on the next couple of days."

In spite of himself, he couldn't help putting his arm around her, pulling her close and kissing the top of her head. "I hope you get some sleep. Don't hesitate to call me if you need me. I'm a light sleeper."

"I won't need you, Jake. Andy's going to be fine. Everything's going to be fine."

He didn't have to be a mind reader to know she was thinking about the adoption again. He hoped her predictions were right on all accounts.

When he left Tori standing by Andy's crib, he wondered if her "I won't need you" declaration was meant to evict him from her life. Maybe throughout this ordeal a few hot kisses and scalding touches were nothing compared to the responsibility she'd taken on. Maybe she could forget about the chemistry between them a lot more easily than he could.

When Jake's bedside phone jangled him awake, from years of habit he sat up, glanced at the clock—3 a.m.—and picked up the receiver. What had gone wrong?

"Hello." His voice was gravelly with the remnants of deep sleep.

"Jake?"

It was Tori, but she didn't sound frantic. She sounded excited. "What is it?"

"It's Andy."

Jake's heart sank. Maybe he'd misread—

"He ate. I've fed him twice, and he kept it down. I think he's really going to be okay."

"You didn't believe his doctor?"

"Oh, Jake, I was so worried."

"I know you were," he said quietly.

"I'm sorry I woke you up. But I just wanted to share the news with you, and the relief."

"I'm glad you did."

"I hope you can go back to sleep."

"If I do go back to sleep, I'll probably dream about you."

His honesty seemed to knock the breath from her.

A few long moments passed before she asked, "Jake? I'm sorry I sent you away the night we danced at the club."

Her honesty almost stopped his heart. But he kept his tone light. "You'd want another dance in your living room?"

"At least a dance."

"And at most?"

He heard her take a breath. "We'll have to decide that when we see each other again."

He thought about their last kiss...about touching her.

"After you're sure Andy's okay, maybe Loretta will baby-sit for a few hours and we can go to my place."

"Jake, I've never had an affair," she said simply. "There hasn't been anyone but Dave."

In a way, Jake felt like swearing a blue streak. A woman who'd never had an affair definitely wanted more than a one-night stand. In the past, he reminded himself again, he'd only been involved with women who didn't want a lasting relationship for very good reasons.

Tori had given him a lot to think about, and he wanted her to think about something, too. "I still don't know if I'll be staying in Santa Fe."

Silence met his statement. Finally she broke it. "I know that. I guess we both have a lot to sleep on. Good night, Jake," she said softly.

''Good night, Tori.''

After Jake hung up, he rubbed his hand over his face, knowing sleep wasn't the answer for the need in his body the phone call had stirred up. He'd get a workout on the bench press in his living room and then he'd go for a run. By the time dawn broke, he might figure out if exploring his desire for Tori would be totally foolhardy—or the smartest thing he'd ever do.

To Tori's surprise, Jake turned up on her doorstep Tuesday evening before she had a chance to phone him again. He held at least four bags of take-out food. In spite of her fatigue, she couldn't help but smile when she saw him, and she opened the door wide so he could come in. ''Something smells wonderful.''

He deposited the bags on her kitchen table. ''I've got Chinese and Italian—*moo goo gai pan,* beef and broccoli, chicken parmesan, linguini and meatballs. Take your pick. When did you last eat?''

For a moment she absolutely could not remember. ''I had breakfast in the cafeteria.''

''That's it all day?''

''Eating just didn't seem important next to bringing Andy home. But I'm hungry now.''

His eyes sparked. ''Good. How's Andy doing?''

''You can see for yourself while I get some plates. Do you want to start a fire and eat in front of the fireplace?''

His voice turned low and husky. ''Sounds like a great idea to me.''

The suggestion had come out of thin air. Or maybe

out of their conversation in the middle of the night. She just knew she didn't want formality with Jake. Or small talk. Or pretense. She was too tired right now to fight the feelings that had started rioting as soon as she'd seen him at her door.

A short time later, she realized Jake wasn't going to pretend the chemistry bubbling between them was a mirage, either. After he'd peeked in on Andy and started a fire, he'd carried the containers of food to the coffee table and settled on the sofa. When she joined him, he patted the cushion next to him.

She sank down beside him, all the tension in her body leaving her at last. She'd been wired for the past few days, worried about Andy. Settled next to Jake, feeling the warmth of his big body, thinking about the moral support he'd given her, she felt the stress of the past week slowly slip away.

They shared the *moo goo gai pan* and the linguini. Most of the time they sat peacefully, gazing at the fire or casting quick glances at each other.

When Jake was finished, he stretched his arm along the back of the sofa. ''What are you going to do about the gallery? Are you going to stay home with Andy? Or hire more help?''

The food and Jake's nearness sent a wonderful, comforting lethargy through Tori. ''I'm not sure. I've actually been thinking about going in for a couple of hours each day and keeping Nina's crib there. I really have to help Loretta get ready for Peter's show.''

She felt Jake's arm stiffen a bit, and she shifted to look up at him. ''Why don't you like Peter?''

''I don't dislike him.''

She arched her brows.

"He's interested in you," Jake said reluctantly.

"He's not simply my client, Jake. We've become friends."

"The same way you and I are friends?"

She and Jake could pretend that was what they were, but more was always brewing under the surface. It always had been. "Definitely not. I'm not attracted to Peter as I am to you."

That seemed to be the signal Jake had been waiting for. His arm descended from the sofa to around her shoulders. With his other hand, he tilted her chin up and gently traced her lips with his thumb. "Are you attracted to him at all?"

"I like Peter. He makes me laugh."

"You also have a lot in common. You move in the same circles. You and I...we're very different."

Feeling those walls Jake wouldn't let crumble, Tori laid her hand on his chest. "Maybe not as different as you think. We care about the same things, Jake. We care about other people...and family. You insist you don't want one, but you're such a natural at it. You're good with kids—"

"And I'm really bad with fairy tales. You've got to accept that, Tori."

Could she accept that he thought marriage was a life sentence? Could she go any further with him, knowing whatever they had would be only temporary? She'd fallen in love with Jake Galeno. She wasn't even sure how or when it had happened. If she knew what they had wasn't permanent, would that help her?

Would her fear that he'd leave go away because she didn't expect him to stay?

He must have seen the doubts and the questions in her eyes. Slowly, he brought his mouth to hers. His kiss was tantalizingly seductive, but he ended it quickly and pulled away. "You enjoy the fire. I'll take the dishes out to the kitchen."

Suddenly she was much too tired to protest. As soon as he stood, she missed the warmth of his body. After he went into the kitchen, she curled up with the pillow, thinking she'd just close her eyes for a few seconds. After that, she didn't remember anything until she felt herself being lifted.

Awakening with a start, she found herself in Jake's arms. "What are you doing?"

"Carrying you to your bedroom."

"I can't go to bed now. I mean—"

He chuckled. "I think you're too worn-out to even consider anything but sleeping."

"I can't sleep. What if Andy wakes up?"

"That's why I'm here. I saw the bottles in the fridge, and I know how to feed a baby. My guess is you haven't slept much for the past few nights, and you need some straight hours desperately."

"Jake, I can't ask you to do this."

At her bedroom now, he pushed the door open with his elbow, carried her to the bed and set her down gently. "You're not asking—I'm offering. Go to sleep, Tori. If anything really important happens, I'll let you know."

Jake's deep voice, the comfortable mattress under her, the softness of her pillow tempted Tori to close her eyes again. After a few deep breaths, the feel of Jake's hand brushing her hair along her cheek, she turned on her side and fell into a dreamland where Jake held her and never let her go.

Chapter Ten

When Tori awoke in the middle of the night to Andy's cry, she immediately sat up. Jake was beside her on the bed on top of the covers.

Reaching over, he touched her shoulder and murmured, ''Go back to sleep. I'll feed him.''

Groggy with sleep, she didn't find it odd that Jake was beside her—not after the dreams she'd had. ''All right. Thank you.''

Once Jake left the bedroom to care for Andy, she undressed, slipped her nightgown on and crawled under the covers. As soon as her head touched the pillow once more, she was asleep with pictures of Jake, Andy and Barbara swirling behind her eyelids.

The following morning when Tori heard the phone beside her ring, she awoke more completely and looked around the room. Jake wasn't anywhere in sight.

The phone stopped after the first ring.

Either someone had the wrong number or Jake had picked up. In the quiet of morning, she heard movement in the living room and the low murmur of Jake's voice. When he didn't come to fetch her, she figured the caller might be Nina.

She glanced at the bedside clock and saw that it was already eight-thirty. Slipping into her robe and belting it, she went to Andy's room and stood by his crib. He was absolutely cherubic, and she felt an overwhelming love that seemed to radiate through her life.

When she found Jake in the kitchen, she noticed a pot of coffee had already been brewed and he was sipping from a steaming mug.

She didn't know where to begin with him. He'd supported her throughout Andy's ordeal. He'd kissed her, but then backed off last night, knowing she was tired. He'd slept beside her in her bed, yet had made no demands. She'd never known a man who'd put her first or cared for her the way Jake had, not to mention caring for her son, too.

Starting with the obvious, she asked, ''Don't you have to be at work?''

''I wanted to make sure you were functioning first.'' He set his mug on the counter with great deliberation and then moved closer to her. With a crooked grin he concluded, ''You look as if you're functioning. How do you feel?''

''More rested than I have in weeks, thanks to you.

I don't know how to thank you, Jake, for everything you've done.''

''I know a good way to start,'' he suggested with a light in his eyes that told her he was going to kiss her.

When his arms went around her, she waited for alarm bells to start clanging, for her common sense to remind her to be careful. Neither happened this morning. As she clasped his shoulders, he pulled her tightly against him, then lowered his head and kissed her cheek, her nose, her neck.

''Jake,'' she murmured, wanting more...wanting everything.

''I have to go to work,'' he said, kissing the skin between the lapels of her robe.

''Andy could wake up any minute,'' she offered, never forgetting about her son, yet needing Jake's kisses.

''We'll only do this for a minute.'' His voice was gravelly and he was breathing harder, just as she was.

His lips took hers then in a demanding kiss, as if they had to reach the depth of passion quickly because their time had run out. When his hands slipped between them to play over the satiny material covering her breasts, her knees felt weak.

A few moments later he dragged out a chair, sat on it and pulled her onto his lap. That way, they could kiss and he could caress her more easily. When his hands slipped under the silky fabric, she'd never before felt sensations so exquisite. His thumb tantalized her nipple, and she moved against his arousal, his shudder telling her that he felt the pleasure, too.

Suddenly he stopped, held her close and laid his

forehead against hers. ‘‘I don’t want our first time to happen like this, grabbed between other things we have to do. I don’t want to have to be somewhere else in fifteen minutes. I don’t want you worrying about Andy waking up. I want to take it slow and easy and make it last.’’

His simple words seemed erotically sensual as pictures danced in her mind—pictures of the two of them in a bed, kissing and touching, joining in an experience she knew she’d never forget. It was like Jake not to want to hurry, to want to squeeze every moment of pleasure out of whatever they did.

Rubbing her cheek against his, telling him she understood, she nodded. ‘‘Okay. But I can’t leave Andy until I’m sure he’s recovered. You understand that, don’t you?’’ She looked up at him, hoping she wouldn’t see impatience or frustration because she was putting her baby first. What she saw was a look so tender it made her want to cry.

‘‘Somehow, I knew you’d say that. We’ll play it by ear,’’ he assured her.

She loved resting against him like this, feeling the beat of his heart, the warmth of his body, the sensual gentleness of him.

She heard a door slam next door, a car start up. Reality snuck in. ‘‘Was that Nina who called? To ask about Andy?’’

She felt Jake’s body tense a bit. ‘‘No. It was Peter Emerson.’’

Straightening on Jake’s lap, she balanced on his legs. ‘‘Why didn’t you tell me?’’

‘‘I *am* telling you.’’

"No. I mean why didn't you come and get me?"

"Because you were sleeping and you needed to sleep."

"Peter is one of my artists, Jake. He knows he can call me at home. You had no right to tamper in my...business dealings."

Hopping from his lap, she belted her robe, now embarrassed by the intimacy they'd shared.

Jake rose, looking annoyed. "I was looking out for you. An hour isn't going to make a difference for you to return his call."

"You don't know that. Just because we..." She wasn't sure what to call what had happened between them. "Just because we're getting closer doesn't mean you have any say in what I do."

As Jake studied her, she felt herself blush. She could see he was thinking about how he'd touched her, how he'd kissed her, and the effect those kisses and touches had had on them both.

"Maybe it's a good thing I have to go to work," he said abruptly, turning to head for the living room.

Feeling thoroughly unsettled, she didn't want him to leave like this. But she didn't know what else to say, either. Finally she decided that being polite was best. "Thank you again for staying last night."

He took his keys from his jeans pocket. "No problem."

He didn't even say goodbye as he left her house, and Tori wondered when she would see him again.

Had she overreacted?

Tori asked herself that question all day and part of

the next. Needing to get out of the house, after supper she drove with Andy to Jake's. But he wasn't home. Frustrated, she took a notepad from her purse and wrote:

> Jake,
>
> I shouldn't have gotten so ruffled yesterday. I'd like to talk about it. I'd love to cook you dinner to thank you for everything you did. If you can make it, come over tomorrow evening about seven. If not, I'll just have leftovers all week.
>
> Tori

She'd tried to keep the tone of her note light, as if mending fences would be easy, as if his acceptance or refusal of dinner didn't matter. But it did. She was feeling things for Jake that scared her. Fear hadn't stopped her after her accident, and fear hadn't stopped her after her divorce. She wasn't going to let fear stop her now.

The following morning, Tori took Andy for his checkup at the doctor's, wondering if Jake would accept her invitation. After she returned home, she fed her baby, and he slept while she prepared tortilla wraps, made a guacamole dip and baked cream puffs for dessert. The pudding would have just enough time to cool.

Andy awoke while she waited for Jake. Her son seemed happier now, more content. She sent up a prayer of thanks again that his surgery had gone well and that he was recovering quickly.

After she bathed him, she cooed to him, played with his little fingers and toes, told him stories about the characters on his revolving mobile, then fed him again and watched him fall asleep. It was almost seven-thirty by then, and she reconciled herself to the fact that she'd be eating dinner alone, trying to tell herself that it was okay if she didn't see Jake anytime soon. But she knew better. He'd settled himself in her heart just as Andy had, and he wasn't budging.

The baby monitor in the kitchen told Tori that Andy was sleeping as she set the oven temperature and slid the tortilla wraps inside. She'd be eating them all week.

When her doorbell rang, her heart beat double-time. She'd dressed in an emerald silk lounging outfit with an oversize shirt and wide-legged trousers. Crossing to the door, she smoothed her hair and took a deep breath.

Jake was wearing a black-and-white Western-cut shirt. The cotton was crisp, as if it was new. His black jeans and boots made him look even taller than his six-two. His thick hair looked damp, as though he'd stepped out of the shower not too long before. In his hand he held a bottle of wine.

With a crooked grin, his gaze slowly passed over her emerald-green outfit. ''Expecting guests?''

''I wasn't sure. I didn't ask for an RSVP.''

His grin slipped away as his expression became serious. ''It didn't matter?''

''It mattered too much,'' she admitted.

The air between them became charged from the

remnants of their argument, the remembered images of their kisses.

Never looking away, he stepped inside.

She took the bottle of wine. "I'll get glasses."

After Jake peeked in on Andy, he came back to the kitchen. "I wish I could sleep that soundly."

"I know what you mean. I'm wondering if I'll ever sleep soundly again. I wake up every once in a while listening for him." She remembered Jake's hand on her shoulder, telling her to go back to sleep, and the secure feeling that she wasn't alone, that she could trust him with her son.

"Mothers are like that."

"I'd bet some fathers are, too."

Mothers and fathers. Partnerships. Parenting together. She was letting herself dream, though she knew that could be dangerous. She turned away from Jake, went to the utility drawer and opened it, looking for a corkscrew.

Before she could find it, she felt him come up behind her. "Tori." Her name on his lips was so seductive her breath caught.

Everything inside of her stilled…waiting. When his arms came around her, she leaned back against him.

"I'm sorry I overreacted."

"I'm sorry I stormed out. I was late tonight because I wasn't sure I should come."

"I'm glad you did," she whispered.

He rubbed his jaw against her hair, and then he kissed her neck. Hot shivers rushed through her limbs. She knew they had to talk. She knew she had to find out if she was dreaming alone. But at that moment,

Andy was asleep, Jake's arms were around her, and all she wanted to feel was him.

"Why don't you turn off the oven?" he murmured in her ear.

His warm breath, the scent of his aftershave, the feel of his lips brushing her skin made coherent thought, let alone action, an impossibility.

"You don't want supper?"

"Food is the furthest thing from my mind." His hands came to rest on her breasts. "What about you?"

"I'm not hungry, either," she whispered, reaching to the back of the stove and switching off the oven. Then she added, "At least not for tortilla wraps."

He turned her into his arms. When she was facing him, he asked, "What *are* you hungry for?"

"You."

"You're so damn honest."

"That's what you like about me," she guessed, managing a smile.

"Only one of the many things." Then his lips were on hers, and like the wind sweeping the desert, pleasure brushed through her, and over her, and was in her.

Each moment seemed suspended in time. She memorized each stroke of his tongue, each surge of his body, each caress that took her somewhere she'd never been.

Breaking the kiss, he stood only far enough away to be able to reach her buttons. Then one by one he unfastened them.

"There are a hell of a lot of these." His tone was a bit ragged.

''You don't have to undo them all. I can just let it drop to the floor.''

That bit of boldness startled him for a moment. Then he gave her a wide grin. ''Good idea.''

His fingers were at her midriff when she stilled his hands, shrugged out of the sleeves and let the silky blouse fall to the tile. When she stepped out of it, she straightened and met his gaze courageously. All of this was so new to her. Dave's ideas about sex had been very traditional. She'd never even thought about letting him undress her in the kitchen. But with Jake, it all seemed natural somehow.

When his fingers traced the lacy straps of her bra, circled the filmy cups, she felt so breathless she didn't know if her pulse would ever be steady again.

Deftly, he reached around her and unfastened her bra. When it dropped away, he took both breasts into his callused hands.

She closed her eyes, loving the feel of his touch. ''Jake,'' she murmured, not knowing how to express what she was feeling.

''I know.'' He rubbed his thumb over her nipple, making every nerve ending in her body tingle. ''I wanted to take this slow, but I don't know if I can.''

''I don't need slow, Jake. I need you.''

With a groan, he stripped off her loose-fitting trousers and panties. She kicked off her sandals. Then she was in his arms. As he kissed her again, he only made it as far as the sofa. After he laid her there, he stripped off his clothes.

She couldn't get enough of looking at him—as his shoulders and chest became bare, as he unbuckled his belt, took off his boots and dropped his jeans. Black hair arrowed down his chest, whorled around his navel and disappeared under the waistband of his briefs. His legs were long, powerfully muscular, hair-roughened, too. He was so virile and so sexy she couldn't wait to feel his naked body against hers.

After he stripped off his briefs, he just stood there, looking at her.

Her heart racing, she asked, "What?"

"I want you, Tori. But I want you to be sure about this."

"I'm sure," she whispered, and held her arms out to him.

After he stretched out on top of her, he held himself up on his forearms, letting their lower bodies become intimately close. Trailing kisses down her cheeks, he then targeted her mouth and throat. Finally his lips were on a breast, his tongue whirling around the nipple.

The heat blooming in her body demanded an outlet. She became restless under him, needing the satisfaction he could bring her. But still he tantalized and teased, not only with his kisses, but with his body, as he rubbed his thighs against hers...probing her most intimate place but not entering...let his hair tease her skin. Her body responded to absolutely everything he was doing. More important, she felt her heart responding, as well. It seemed to overflow with her newfound love for Jake, and with her hopes and dreams and longings. Ever since her accident she'd felt inadequate and less of a woman. But as Jake stroked and petted, taking their passion to a whole new level, she'd never felt more fully a woman.

When his hands slipped between her thighs, she sucked in a breath. "I want to make sure you're ready." His voice was thick with his own need.

"I'm ready." She'd been ready for him for years. Long ago, her heart had chosen him. She realized that now. A master plan had brought them back together, and she felt as if being with Jake now was the most right thing she'd ever done.

Just as he'd reached down to see if she was ready, she took him in her hands. "I want to make you feel good, too."

His deep chuckle was self-deprecating. "If I felt any better, we'd be in real trouble."

Still, she held him, stroked him and felt the pulsing beat. He was so alive. So emphatically male. So hungry.

"Now, Tori." His voice was a growl.

Sliding her arms around his back, she stroked the sleek muscles and dug her fingers into his backside. "Yes. Now."

She called Jake's name in a ragged moan as he entered her. Her body was tight and he took his time, giving them both excruciating pleasure. Their bodies seemed to melt into each other as their breaths mingled. Jake's kiss was as thoroughly claiming as his presence inside her. Passion coiled between them... radiated out...wrapped them in heat, and abandon, and a joining that rocked her existence. Their rhythm took on a primitive drumbeat cadence, the same cadence she sensed when she ventured into the mountains she loved so much. Suddenly she could hear the chant of all the women who had come before her, and in a rush of self-awareness, she knew who she was, what her place was, where she belonged. She belonged with Jake.

His thrusts became more potent, went deeper. She wrapped her legs around him, reveling in the desire that had always pulsed between them. She wanted their union to go on forever. Waves of inexorable pleasure rippled and roared around her. She withstood them, reaching for more.

Jake gave her more.

Finally she knew she couldn't prolong the pleasure. She had to give in to it. Jake swept her with him, from desert to snowy mountaintop. They were suspended there for a timeless second until the world burst around them. She felt tears fall down her cheeks as Jake called her name.

Moments later, Jake eased to the back of the sofa, still joined to her, holding her tight.

When their breathing had become more normal, she teased, "We could move to the bed. Then you wouldn't have to protect me from falling off the sofa."

He chuckled. "The bed? If we head there, we might never have dinner."

"I don't care," she said honestly.

He looked down on her. "Yes, you do. You care a lot, about everything. That's what worries me about this."

This. Jake thought of them as "this." The hopes and dreams that had floated like clouds around a mountaintop evaporated and she was faced with reality. Jake had told her many times how he felt about a serious relationship and marriage. He wanted no part of them.

"Where do we go from here?" she asked quietly.

"That depends on you. And what you want for Andy."

She made a sudden decision that she knew was going to cause her nothing but heartache. But heartache was part of life, and she loved Jake too much to send him away. "I want to be with you now. You don't know where you're headed. I don't know what tomorrow's going to bring. Let's just take this day by day."

"That sounds like a fine idea to me."

"My mom and her friend will be arriving next week. While they're here..."

He tipped her chin up. "I'll understand if you're busy. As you said, we'll take everything day by day."

Tori knew Jake was satisfied with *now.* But she wanted *forever.* Deep down she realized that that difference would tear them apart. But at the moment Jake was holding her and she was holding him.

It was enough. For now.

"This is Sean." Sylvia Phillips introduced the man who had traveled with her to Santa Fe.

Tori had offered to pick up her mother and Sean Brady at the Albuquerque International Sunport. But her mom had claimed the airport was easy to navigate, and they wanted to rent a car to see a few sights and to travel freely while they were here. They'd checked in at the bed-and-breakfast a few blocks away. When they'd called to tell Tori they'd arrived, Tori had insisted they come over for dinner.

As her mother stood in Tori's living room now, she looked more glowing than Tori had ever seen her. Her ash-brown hair, wavy and cut to frame her face, looked highlighted. That was new. She was wearing makeup, too—lipstick, eye shadow, a bit of mascara. Her mother had never bothered before with anything but lipstick. Her slim figure was as trim as ever in denim slacks and a denim jacket embroidered with abstract cats. She looked much younger than her fifty-five years, and Tori supposed the new youthfulness was thanks to the man beside her—Sean Brady.

The tall, husky Irishman extended his hand to Tori. "It's good to meet you. I feel like I know you. Your mom has talked so much about you."

The man's grip was as sturdy as he was. "It's good to meet you, too, Mr. Brady," Tori said politely, withdrawing her hand from his.

Apparently Sean didn't want to let formality stand between them. "It's Sean. I know you and your mom want to spend time together while she's here. If I get in the way, just tell me to take a hike. I've got a map and plenty of bottled water. Before we came, I surfed the Net for everything I want to see.

"On the other hand," he maintained, his green eyes twinkling, "I'll be glad to be included whenever you want me around. I especially want to see this baby boy you and your mom jabber about on the phone. It's a shame he's had such a rough time of it."

In spite of her misgivings, Tori felt herself warming toward her mother's friend. She couldn't seem to grasp the fact that her mother had a lover. "Andy's sleeping right now, but we can take a peek if you'd like."

Smiling, Sylvia looped her arm through Sean's. "We'd like. I can't wait to see my grandson."

As Tori led the way, she felt such joy and such pride to be introducing her son to her mother. The three of them stood at the crib silently for a few minutes. Finally Sylvia rested her fingers on the baby's leg. "He's so precious."

Tori could hear the emotion in her mother's voice, and she felt tears prick her eyes, too.

Finally the women tiptoed toward the door.

"I think I'll just stay and watch him a while," Sean said. "I promise I won't wake him. But if he shows signs of wanting some company, I'll come and get you."

Tori smiled as her mother followed her into the hall. When they passed the bathroom, her mom caught sight of the changes. "Isn't this beautiful!"

She stepped inside and gazed all around, examining the tiles, the floor, the new light. "And your friend did all this?"

Suddenly Tori caught sight of a lone black sock dragging on the floor near the hamper. It wasn't hers. In her rush to straighten up, take care of Andy and make supper, she'd missed it.

Now her mother walked over to the hamper and stooped down beside it. When she lifted the sock, there was a grin on her face. "You can't tell me this is one of yours. Your feet are a lot smaller."

"No. No, it's not one of mine. I've been seeing someone."

"It must be serious if he's leaving his socks." When Sylvia analyzed Tori's expression, her own became serious. "You didn't tell me anything about it."

"Probably for the same reason you didn't tell me about Sean. I'm not certain about anything."

"Have you known him long?"

"I met Jake when I was in high school. He took me to my prom, remember?"

Sylvia nodded. "Nina Galeno's brother."

"That's right. Our lives crossed again about two months ago. He's the one who did the tile work."

"And already there are socks on your floor? You can't tell me you know a man in that amount of time."

"I know Jake. As soon as you meet him, you realize there aren't many men like him. He's honorable and strong."

"But?"

"But his life's unsettled right now and he doesn't have a high opinion of marriage."

"You haven't had a high opinion of marriage, either. That's my fault."

"No. It's my father's fault and Dave's fault."

After a long pause, her mom asked, "What do you think of Sean?"

"I just met him."

"I know. But what's your first impression?"

Tori took her mother's hand and gave it a squeeze. "He seems very nice. Very caring. Very honest. Ask me before you leave and I'll give you a better assessment."

"When do I get to meet this...Jake?"

"Tonight. I asked him to come over for dinner, but

he thought the three of us should have this time alone. He'll be here around eight."

Sunday, the day of Andy's christening, dawned bright with a hint of winter in the air. Jake enjoyed the ceremony, the solemnity and the celebration afterward more than he'd enjoyed anything in a long while. During the week before Sylvia Phillips had arrived, he'd stayed over every night at Tori's and they had gotten little sleep. Since her mother had come to town, he hadn't spent much time alone with Tori. He missed her in more than a physical way.

The party at Tori's house after the christening had been noisy and crowded. But eventually Nina, Charlie, Jake's mom and the boys had left. For the past few days, Jake had felt as if he'd gotten to know Sylvia and Sean. He liked them both. But he sensed a slight wariness whenever they looked at him, and he wondered what Tori had told them about their relationship.

As Jake watched Sylvia rocking Andy, tickling his chin, playing with his baby fingers, she glanced at him and their gazes locked. What *was* she thinking? That her daughter was foolish to begin an affair that had nowhere to go?

A knife twisted in Jake's gut when he thought about ending it. Whenever he held Tori in his arms, he felt a peace he hadn't experienced since Marion's death. His desire for Tori hadn't eased since they'd had sex. It had grown stronger. Every time she was around, the strength of his desire amazed him. But he also felt cornered by it. He didn't want to need her any more than she wanted to need him. He just wanted to walk away from this when it was over with his psyche still intact.

And it *would* be over, at some point. Tori would want more than pleasure a few nights a week. Then he'd walk away. Commitment took too much, demanded too much, destroyed too much.

"If you gentlemen don't mind," Tori said with a smile, "Mom and I are going to give Andy a bath."

"They're more fun when they start splashing," Sean informed her.

"Tori's already bought toys for the bathtub for when that day comes," Jake said with a chuckle.

As the two women went down the hall, Sean slid to the edge of the sofa and leaned closer to Jake. In a lowered voice he asked, "Are you serious about Tori?"

"That depends on what you mean by serious," Jake answered casually, suspecting Sylvia and Sean had discussed this subject often the past few days.

Instead of jumping on him because he didn't give a straight answer, Sean frowned. "I know what Tori's father put her mom through. Tori saw it all. She saw her mother find another woman's earring in the car. She saw Sylvia take Eric back when he apologized time after time. She saw her mom go into a deep depression when he left. It got so bad Tori finally went to one of her neighbors for help—her mom hadn't gotten out of bed for days, and she thought Sylvia was going to die."

"Tori never told me that," Jake admitted.

"From what Sylvia says, Tori doesn't give much away. From what I gathered, that husband of hers really did a number on her, too. But Sylvia says you'd never know it, because Tori held her head high through the whole thing.''

''Why are you telling me this?''

''I'm telling you this because I'm going to marry Sylvia, and I'm going to be Tori's stepfather. She'll be part of my family, and I take care of my own. If you're not serious, I don't want you leading her on. Just thought we'd cover the bases now.''

Sean Brady had covered the bases, all right. Jake had told himself over and over again he should get out of Tori's life before he hurt her. She'd made it obvious she didn't want to depend on him. She'd made it obvious she didn't want to need him. But in her bed in the black of night, they somehow let go of defenses, tore down walls and united in a way he'd never united with a woman before.

Still, the black of night wasn't going to be enough for Tori. Someday soon, probably after Andy's adoption was finalized, she'd turn to someone like Peter Emerson. And Jake would move on to another place...to another woman, who didn't care about tomorrow any more than he did.

Chapter Eleven

Tori absolutely sparkled, Jake thought, as he stood beside a large framed canvas, watching her across the expanse of her gallery. She was wearing an off-the-shoulder, jewel-toned dress that glittered with beads embroidered in an intricate design. The hem fell just above her knees, and the dress was form-fitting enough for him to see the curves he'd caressed…curves he'd stroked…curves that had him as hot as blazes here in the midst of an art show. Her swingy, glittering earrings had to be diamonds. Every once in a while he glimpsed one when her hair swayed. She was talking to her mother, gesturing toward one of Peter Emerson's paintings, as Sean looked on.

Jake smiled. The Irishman was clearly bored. Since Sean hadn't brought along anything formal, he'd gone out and bought a Western shirt and sprung for a bolo tie.

Jake realized his own shirt collar was feeling tight. It had been a while since he'd worn a suit.

When Emerson walked up to Tori and touched her elbow, Jake's teeth clenched. Suddenly he felt a hand on his shoulder.

"Why the frown?" Phil Trujillo asked.

"I think I tied my tie too tight," Jake answered with an expression that said his frown was none of Trujillo's business.

Phil looked at Tori and Emerson. "Mm-hm. I saw you with Tori Phillips earlier. You look good together."

Although annoyance niggled at Jake, his tone was calm. "What are you doing here? Art shows aren't exactly your gig."

"Maybe I'm having my consciousness raised."

At that Jake chuckled. "Sure. Now tell me something I'll believe."

Trujillo gave a shrug. "Just checking things out. I have a composite sketch I want to show Ms. Phillips."

"You've ID'd a suspect?"

"Nope. Mrs. Cranshaw at the bakery told me she saw a guy hanging around the parking lot a couple of times. So I set her up with a sketch artist." He pulled a folded sheet of paper from an inside pocket and showed it to Jake.

"I've never seen him before."

Trujillo tucked the sketch back into his pocket. "I'll wait till this is all over, maybe bring the sketch by in the morning. I wouldn't want to throw a wrench into Ms. Phillips's evening.''

''If you're going to hang around, you must have a reason.''

''You never know where our suspect will turn up. If he has balls, or no sense, he might think this show is a good way to look around the place firsthand.''

''You think he's still in the area?''

''There's no way of knowing. Just to be on the safe side, I thought I'd cover this tonight.''

The hum of voices and clink of glasses were background noises as Jake said, ''I didn't appreciate Chief Garcia's visit or the fact that you told him where he could find me.''

Trujillo grinned and shrugged. ''How do you know I told him? The chief has his ways of finding out what he wants to know. He likes your record.''

''Lay off, Phil.''

''If you say so.''

The quick reply made Jake cast a sideways glance at the detective. He knew that Phil could bluff with the best of them.

When Phil moved away, Sean wandered over to Jake. He jerked a thumb back at the six-foot-high canvas where Sylvia was standing. ''You get that stuff?''

Jake slipped his hand into his pocket. His fingers played with the key Tori had given him to the back door of the gallery. He'd picked up, then delivered a few easels she'd purchased to display Emerson's paintings. Now he couldn't suppress a smile at Sean's question. ''I probably get it as much as you do. Personally, I like art that's more realistic.''

"Exactly. I don't want to have to figure out whether it's a horse or a house or a tree. But Sylvia seems to enjoy all this as much as Tori." He pointed to one of Emerson's smaller paintings. "I might buy her that as a wedding gift."

Tori hadn't mentioned that anything had been finalized between her mother and Sean Brady. "Have you set a date?"

"It's a secret," Sean admitted, his eyes twinkling. "We're going to announce it officially at Christmas. I think we've convinced Tori to fly out with Andy. Are you going to come along?"

Christmas was almost two months away. Jake didn't know where he and Tori would be by then. "I'll check my schedule," he said diplomatically. "But whether I'm there or not, I wish you and Mrs. Phillips all the best."

Tori was speaking to a group of three couples. She had a glass of champagne in her hand, but Jake didn't think she'd taken a sip all evening. He suspected it was more for show than anything else. She was celebrating Peter Emerson's success and wanted to let him and everyone else know it. Emerson, on the other hand, had downed at least three glasses and was thoroughly enjoying himself, explaining the intimate details of his work to a prospective buyer.

As the couples drifted away from Tori, she was finally standing alone for the first time all evening.

Sean's gaze had followed Jake's. "I'm going to see if Sylvia wants another glass of champagne."

Jake had missed Tori the past five days. Most of her time had been taken up by her mom and Sean.

Jake didn't begrudge her any of that. The truth was, he'd felt out of place as Sean snoozed on the sofa in the evenings while Sylvia and Tori bathed and fed Andy. Sylvia couldn't seem to hold him enough or coo to him enough or rock him enough. Jake understood that, too. But he'd felt as if he didn't have any place there.

He didn't. He wasn't Andy's father.

Another man approached Tori. Tall and loose-limbed, he appeared to be in his middle forties. He seemed to know her, and they had a conversation that lasted almost five minutes. She was smiling, animated, and even blushed a little.

Jake felt himself tense. Suddenly he realized he wasn't jealous of Peter Emerson or of the man talking to Tori now. After all, Jake was the one sleeping with her. *He* was the one who knew she liked long, deep kisses. *He* was the one who knew what made her sigh or moan with pleasure. What he felt when he saw Emerson, or any other man, with her was a deep abiding sadness that she didn't belong to him, wouldn't belong to him, because he couldn't tell her he'd stay.

Do you really want to be a partner in a lodge in Crested Butte? a reasonable voice inside him asked.

On the nights when he stayed with Tori, when he lost himself in her, when her touches and her welcoming body gave him release that rocked his world, he thought of Crested Butte, a more isolated life and peace of mind he couldn't seem to find anywhere. He needed Tori on a level beyond the physical. Yet that need disturbed him, unsettled him, trapped him. The same way his father had felt trapped?

Couldn't be. He and Tori didn't have a commitment to each other. They didn't have any plans for the future.

But they had a bond, one Jake couldn't deny. It went beyond the passion, beyond Andy's birth and his surgery. It was a bond Jake didn't understand.

He'd had a bond with Marion. Maybe he'd never been able to admit it before. They'd had a professional relationship and a friendship. He'd been her superior, her teacher, her mentor. He'd never acted on the attraction he'd felt for her, and she'd never admitted that she'd come to him to ask for his advice more than necessary.

He'd been attracted to her, he'd cared for her, and he'd sent her to her death.

He had to resolve his guilt. He had to get past the recriminations. He had to get over what had happened before he could consider anything more permanent with Tori than going to bed with her tonight and waking up beside her in the morning.

As if Tori could sense his turmoil, she looked his way. Their gazes locked, and he started moving toward her. She finished her conversation and met him in the middle of the gallery, stopping by a table laden with hors d'oeuvres.

"Have you eaten yet tonight?" he asked her.

"I haven't been hungry. Too much to do, too many people to talk to. That was a reporter who wants to interview Peter."

"You, too?"

She nodded. "He's coming tomorrow morning around ten."

"What time is your mom leaving?"

"Around 6 a.m. We'll have to say our goodbyes tonight."

"Have you checked in with Nina?" Since Loretta was involved in this show as much as Tori, his sister had offered to baby-sit Andy.

"About half an hour ago. Andy had his bottle at seven and has been sleeping ever since."

Jake knew Tori had come to the gallery around four to help get the evening set up and make sure everything was just as it should be. "I've missed you," he said honestly.

A patron brushed by Tori and she almost spilled her champagne. The gallery was more crowded than it had been all evening. "I've missed you, too," Tori confessed.

Impulsively, Jake took her hand. "Come on."

"Where are we going?"

He tugged her toward the back of the gallery. "We're going to steal a few moments alone. Any objections?"

Her aquamarine eyes sparked with the same need that he felt. "Not at all."

After Jake tugged Tori into the storage room, they laughed like a couple of kids who had just escaped a truant officer. Tori set her champagne glass on a stack of boxes. Then Jake took her into his arms and their laughter dwindled away.

"It's been too long," he said. "I'm going to mess up your lipstick."

"I don't care," she returned recklessly, and he could see that she really had missed him, too. When their lips met, the storage room became their world. Art patrons, Peter Emerson, champagne and hors d'oeuvres were forgotten as their need consumed them both. Jake's hands roamed all over her, reveled in the smooth texture of her skin. He was frustrated by material and beads. When her hand slid under his jacket, he wanted to undress her right then and there.

"How long do you think we have until someone comes looking for us?" he asked, half joking, half serious.

"About two minutes." Her smile said she regretted it as much as he did.

"That long?" he teased. "I don't think I can work wonders in two minutes."

Laughing, she pressed tighter against him. "I think you're ready to try."

Groaning, he nipped her neck. "Better watch it, or everyone will know what we've been doing out here."

"Counting my inventory."

"Counting the minutes until I can take you to bed again."

"You'll stay tonight?"

"I'll stay." Yes, tonight. Maybe tomorrow night. He wouldn't think beyond that.

The following afternoon, Tori carefully packaged the painting that Sean wanted to buy for her mother. Strains of Native American flute instrumentals played in the background. Sean had confided the artwork was going to be his wedding present to Sylvia and then had waited for Tori's reaction. To her surprise, after only a few days of knowing Sean, she'd taken the news easily. She really liked the man. He seemed to add excitement and caring and tenderness to her mother's life. The same elements Jake could add to hers. For the past week, thoughts of a wedding band on her finger again hadn't seemed so extraordinary.

A little gurgle came from Andy as he sat in his car seat on the counter where she was working. He was such a contented baby now. She was sure that his little smiles weren't accidents, that he actually recognized her voice, her touch. Was that possible at seven weeks?

''When you're finished with that, I'll take it to the post office for you,'' Loretta offered as she carried artwork from the storage area into the gallery. They had sold so many of Peter's paintings that they had to rearrange them now and fill the spaces with other artists' work.

''I'd appreciate that. I'm going to meet Jake at the toy store after the gallery closes. We have to buy birthday presents for his nephews.''

''Need a sitter for Andy?''

Tori laughed. ''Nope. I'm taking him along this evening. I have bottles in the fridge in back. He'll probably sleep while we shop.''

Loretta came around the counter and gave the rattle attached to the seat a little shake. When the baby responded to the movement, she smiled. ''I hope your mother and Sean have a smooth flight home. With all the commotion this morning, we hardly had a minute to breathe, let alone talk.''

Shortly after Tori and Loretta had opened the gallery today, Detective Trujillo had come in with his composite sketch. Tori had been sure she'd never seen the thick-necked man in the sketch before. Loretta was less sure. She thought he resembled a customer who'd come in the previous week asking about upcoming art shows. She'd given him brochures on Peter's show, as well as Renée Ludwig's, which would be held the Tuesday before Thanksgiving. Detective Trujillo had asked several more questions, reminded them both that the person sketched might simply be a frequent customer of the shops in the small plaza, and then left.

Soon after, Peter had arrived and so had the journalist for *Around Santa Fe,* a quarterly magazine that would give the artist terrific exposure. The interview had lasted until lunch. Tori had mostly listened, fed Andy in a chair close by and made sure he was settled for his morning nap in Nina's portable crib. Bringing him to the gallery when she needed to oversee matters herself didn't seem to be a problem. Once he started crawling and walking, maybe she could hire more help and arrange coming into the gallery one day a week.

She'd definitely have to hire additional staff within the next few weeks before Christmas, especially if she and Andy were going to visit her mother and Sean in Kansas. She hadn't yet asked Jake if he'd come along.

Running tape around the edges of the box that held the painting safely ensconced in bubble wrap, she mused aloud, "I want to find something really unique for a wedding present for my mom and Sean. They both have everything they need."

"Something simple might please your mom more than something elaborate. Did you take pictures while they were here?"

''Loads of them.''

''You could do a collage, then mat and frame it.''

Jake would appear in lots of those pictures. Tori ached to have him in her life permanently. ''That's a wonderful idea. I'm sure Mom would appreciate that more than anything I could buy.''

When the bell on the door rang, Tori looked up and then went perfectly still. Barbara Simmons had just walked in, her expression serious. She'd lost much of the weight she'd gained during her pregnancy. Her gaze landed directly on Andy.

Tori didn't move from Andy's side, but she smiled warmly. ''Hi, Barbara. It's good to see you.''

''My mom said you called. Andrew was sick?''

''He was. But he's not sick anymore. He had to have surgery.'' Tori explained what condition had developed and how the doctor had remedied it.

Barbara couldn't seem to take her eyes off Andy. ''He's grown so much.''

''Yes, he has. Inches and pounds. How was your trip?''

As Loretta moved away, Barbara shrugged. ''It was okay. It was fun to be with Vanessa and Melanie again.''

''They're not going to college?''

''Melanie's starting in January, like I am. Her grades weren't good enough to get her into the fall session. Vanessa's not sure what she wants to do. Her parents just got divorced and she's pretty messed up over that. She's trying to get her head together. She plays in an all-girl band and has these dreams of becoming a star. She has an aunt in California, and she's thinking about going out there and looking around.''

Watching Barbara and listening to her, Tori thought the teenager seemed more subdued than she'd ever seen her.

Barbara reached out and gently stroked Andy's hair. The little boy looked up at her. ''It wasn't the same as before,'' she said in a low voice.

''What wasn't the same?''

''Being with them. I thought everything would go back to being the way it was. You know—before I got pregnant and all. But they're so into guys and clothes...''

''And you're not?''

''A guy is the last thing I want to think about. They just laughed when I said I wanted to be a neurosurgeon. Vanessa said it'll never work because I might chip a nail. But I don't care about things like that anymore.''

''What do you care about?'' Tori asked softly.

''Different stuff. I just kept thinking that I only held Andy once. I didn't know if you'd be here. I didn't think he'd be here. Would it be all right...would it be all right if I picked him up?''

Tori's insides were gyrating, and the fears that had become tempered over the past couple of weeks came fully awake. Still, she knew she had to let this teenager say goodbye to her baby, since she obviously hadn't done that. ''Of course you can pick him up. Just make sure you keep his head supported.''

Gathering up Andy, Barbara was careful as she put

him to her shoulder. Her face was close to his and she swayed back and forth a little. ''He smells good.''

''Not all the time,'' Tori joked, trying not to let panic run away with her.

Barbara turned away then, looking around the gallery. She slowly began walking around with Andy, becoming more sure of herself.

Tori made herself wait by the counter.

It was only a few minutes, but it seemed like an eternity before Barbara brought Andy back, placed him in his car seat again and picked up her purse. ''I have to go. Thanks for letting me hold him.''

Not sure what to say or do, Tori kept silent.

Barbara smiled weakly. ''See you the week after next. My lawyer will call you with the time and place.'' Then she hurried out the gallery door.

Lifting Andy, Tori held him close, praying her fears were figments of her imagination and Barbara would sign the final papers, hoping the teenager would get on with her life and forget about her son.

When Jake picked up Tori at the gallery, she still felt unsettled by Barbara's visit. But she pushed it from her mind, eager to enjoy this time with Jake. Andy's car seat was positioned in the back seat of Jake's cab. Since the seat faced backward, she couldn't see Andy when she looked over her shoulder. Jake could, though.

''He's fine,'' he assured her. ''Will this be the first time he's ridden in his stroller?''

''No. I've taken him for a few walks. He seems to like it.''

"Babies always like movement," Jake said with a chuckle.

As they parked at the entrance to the toy store, Tori asked, "What do you want to buy the boys?"

"Not videos. I want to get them some good, old-fashioned toys that will make them use their imaginations. Maybe some books, too."

"Just what are old-fashioned toys?" Tori asked with a smile.

"Maybe one of those big fire engines. I don't want to get them both the same thing, so maybe I can get that for Ricky and find a construction truck for Ryan."

"They won't fight over each other's?"

Jake grinned. "Probably. But they'll learn how to share, too."

They took a few moments to unfold the stroller and settle Andy in it. Then Jake wheeled it across the parking lot and lifted it over the curb. When they went inside, he pushed it like a proud dad.

Tonight she'd ask him to go with her to her mother's at Christmas.

This time of year the toy store was busy. Clerks were adding stock to the shelves, unpacking boxes, directing parents already looking for bargains for Christmas. Tori took over steering the stroller while Jake commandeered a cart. It didn't take him long to find exactly what he wanted.

He loaded the trucks into the cart. Tori picked up two small remote-controlled cars, knowing the boys would get a kick out of them, and dropped them into the basket.

Tossing her a smile, Jake headed for the sporting-goods section. ''Charlie said something about buying them a football. I'll get them a basketball. They'll probably want a hoop set up before they're too much older.''

''*They'll* want a hoop or *you* want a hoop?''

He grinned and plucked a basketball from the shelf, examining it closely. ''There's not much difference right now. While I'm here—''

''Jake Galeno!''

Jake's name was a startled cry, coming from a woman who had just turned into the aisle and spotted him. She was petite, with short brown hair streaked with gray. She wore a long broomstick skirt in brown and green. Her overblouse was also green and she carried a jacket over one arm.

Dropping the basketball into the cart, Jake straightened. ''Hello, Mrs. Montgomery.''

''That's all you have to say to me? Hello?''

''There's so much I'd like to say, but I don't think this is the place. I'm so sorry about Marion. You've got to know that.''

''I don't know anything anymore. My lawyer said I couldn't sue you or the police department, that there was no wrongdoing. But I don't care what your Internal Affairs said. Someone was to blame. You trained Marion. You put her in that situation. You should have been in there instead of her.''

Tori could see the pain in Jake's eyes and on his face. She didn't know what this was all about, but whatever it was, it was the reason he was in Santa Fe. It was the reason he had left the police force in Albuquerque. It was obvious Mrs. Montgomery was more than grief-stricken. She was angry down to her soul.

"She was just a novice in negotiation," the woman went on. "She didn't know how to handle herself. You got her killed!"

Jake's face was drawn, and when he spoke, Tori could hear the anguish he'd obviously experienced since the incident had happened. "You can't blame me any more than I blame myself."

His comment seemed to take the woman by surprise. If she was expecting a righteous justification, Jake obviously didn't intend to give it.

"I'd like to talk to you sometime, someplace other than here."

"I don't want an explanation for what happened. My baby is dead. I just want her back." With that, Mrs. Montgomery spun around and fled down the aisle.

Tori and Jake stood in silence as the loudspeaker crackled and shoppers continued their searches, as if nothing earth-shattering had occurred.

"Are you okay?" Tori asked.

A guardedness came over him, the guardedness that she'd seen slowly drop away over the past few weeks. "I'm fine."

"Maybe we should go. If you want to talk about it—"

"I don't want to talk about it, Tori. Talking about it only makes it worse. Let's just finish shopping and get out of here."

Jake headed for the book aisle so fast Tori could

hardly keep up. Why couldn't he let his walls down? Why couldn't he tell her what had happened?

One look at Jake's stony face said he didn't need help picking out books for Ricky and Ryan. She'd no sooner chosen one for Andy when Jake asked, "Ready to go?"

She was ready to leave the store, go back to her house and get some explanations. She simply nodded and followed him to the checkout line.

In the cab of the truck once more, with Andy safely tucked into his car seat, Tori offered, "I can make something at the house. Maybe an omelette."

He switched on the ignition. "I won't be coming in tonight."

"Jake—"

"I'm not in the mood for questions. And I know you're going to ask them."

"What if I promise not to?"

"It won't last. We'll eat supper, feed Andy, go to bed, and eventually you'll ask."

"Maybe then you'll be ready to—"

"No." He shifted gears, let off the brake and headed for the street.

Ten minutes later, he'd carried Andy inside for her, retrieved the stroller and her shopping bag from the truck and said good-night.

She clasped his arm. "Don't go like this, Jake."

"I just need to be alone, Tori. Try to understand that."

But she didn't understand. She didn't understand why he was becoming her world and she didn't fit in to his.

* * *

Tori was straightening up her living room while Andy watched from his stroller. She'd put on a CD of children's songs. As she sang along, she dusted, smiled at her son and tickled him now and then. He seemed to enjoy all of it. She just wished...

She wished Jake was sharing every moment of this. She hadn't heard from him since their trip to the toy store the night before last. She thought about calling him. But if he needed space, she had to give it to him. Didn't she?

Tori had gone back to dusting when her phone rang. Taking the stroller with her, she rushed to it, hoping it was Jake. "Hello."

"Tori, it's Tom Davidson."

It was her lawyer. He was probably calling to tell her the place and time when Barbara would sign the final papers. Maybe Barbara's lawyer had contacted him. "Hi, Tom. Do you have the arrangements made for signing the final papers?"

The silence that met her words warned her there was trouble. "Barbara Simmons's lawyer called me."

Tori's heart stopped. She couldn't even ask the obvious questions.

"Barbara wants to take Andy for the weekend."

"What do you mean, take him?"

"She's having doubts about the adoption. Her mother is going to be away, and she wants to take Andy and care for him herself."

"You've got to be kidding."

"I'm afraid not, Tori. You're his legal guardian, but eighteen or not, she's his mother."

"Can't we stop this?"

"*You* could. But what good would that do? If we don't let her take him for the weekend, she certainly won't sign the papers."

"Oh, Tom."

"I know. This is tough. But you knew it might happen. It could just be part of a necessary process. Don't give up hope."

"When…when does she want Andy?"

"She said if it's all right with you, she'll pick him up this afternoon around four. Do you want her to come to my office?"

"No. That doesn't make any sense. She can pick him up here."

"If you don't want any contact with her, I can handle it."

"Contact doesn't make any difference at this point. I'm not going to turn hysterical. If you want to be here, that's fine."

"It would probably be a good idea. I'd like to document everything that happens for the judge."

Tori listened to the rest of her conversation with Tom in a heart-hurting haze. After her lawyer clicked off, she stared at the keypad on the phone, and then she dialed Jake's number.

Chapter Twelve

Jake had kept himself busy, trying to put the encounter with Marion's mother out of his mind, trying to forget the questions he'd seen in Tori's eyes. Questions he hadn't wanted to answer. He didn't *have* answers.

And he certainly didn't want to rehash everything that had happened. Yet when Tori had called him to tell him Barbara was taking Andy for the weekend, he'd felt as if he'd been poleaxed, too, and could only imagine what was going through Tori's head.

Working through his lunch hour to leave the job early, he pulled up in front of Tori's in time to see Barbara standing on the porch with Andy in her arms. Tori stood in the doorway with the man who must be her lawyer. Her face was drawn and her arms were wrapped around herself.

As Jake approached, he could see her knuckles were white. He could only imagine her anguish as she thought about never seeing the baby she wanted as her son again. This visit could mean the adoption was off. Her voice had trembled as she'd told Jake that earlier. Then she'd taken a breath, composed herself and said she just thought he might want to know.

Damn, yes, he wanted to know! He wasn't about to let her go through this alone.

Although Barbara's face was pale, too, and her eyes bright, there was resolution in her stance as she held her baby. "I'll bring him back Sunday night, no matter what I decide. I promise."

Jake understood exactly what Barbara meant. If she was going to keep her baby, Tori would have another week with him.

"Do you have a car seat?" Tori asked, her voice surprisingly normal.

"Yes, I do. I borrowed it from a friend of my mom's. I have formula and diapers and everything else I'll need, too."

Jake wondered about that. There was more resolution on Barbara's face than the motherly concern he always saw on Tori's. That wasn't fair, he guessed, because Barbara hadn't had time to bond with her child. Still, when Tori had first seen Andy, there'd been no doubt what she felt.

Barbara's gaze met Jake's, then she looked away and hurried to her car.

The scene seemed frozen in time. The three of them didn't move, but rather watched as Barbara strapped Andy into the car seat and drove away.

Tori gave Jake a weak smile, then turned and went inside the house. When Jake and the lawyer joined her, she introduced them.

"It's going to be a long weekend," she said, letting out a huge breath.

Her lawyer, a gray-haired man in his fifties, looked at her kindly. "I could still have the judge make Barbara return that baby to you."

"But only temporarily. If she doesn't sign the final papers, he's hers again. As you told me, I'm cornered, Tom. There's nothing I can do but wait and see what she decides."

"I suggest you not sit around here all weekend. You'll make yourself crazy."

"I could go into the gallery—"

Jake interrupted. "I have a better idea. Let me make a call."

Tori's gaze was curious as he went into the kitchen for a little privacy.

Ten minutes later when he returned to the living room, Tori's lawyer had left and she was sitting on the sofa sorting through a pack of pictures she'd recently had developed. He suspected most of them were of Andy.

"If you want to get away from here, I have a place we can go. An old friend of mine has a *casita* near Chimayo he rarely uses. It's rustic, but it has electricity and running water. We could go hiking tomorrow. You could make yourself so tired you might be able to sleep at night."

"You don't have to give up your weekend for me, Jake. I just wanted you to know what was happening, since you were there when Andy was born, and…'' Her voice trailed off, and he remembered exactly where they'd left things.

Closing the distance between them, he stood very close but didn't touch her. ''I care about what happens to you and Andy. You *will* make yourself crazy if you stay here. Even if you go into the gallery and work, it won't take your mind off Barbara. But physical exertion might. We can even drive over to White Rock Overlook and Bandelier to explore the cliff dwellings. Whatever it takes to make the time pass.''

He knew Tori found strength in the mountains. Nothing was more spectacular than standing at the Overlook, gazing down at gorges and waterfalls. And the cliff dwellings at Bandelier—they would take her out of the present, thrust her into the past and maybe help her forget for a short while.

''If I leave and Barbara needs to reach me—''

''You have your cell phone.''

''The mountains could interfere.''

Now he did take Tori by the shoulders, then rubbed his thumbs along her cheekbones. ''You can call in for messages. We can always find a land line.'' Nudging her chin up, he saw the questions in her vulnerable blue-green eyes. ''We'll just take each hour as it comes.''

The urge to hold her and kiss her and make love to her was so strong he fought the desire with every ounce of self-control he possessed. There was a world of difference between them, a past he couldn't shake and too much riding on what would happen with the baby for him to give in to more primitive instincts.

"Go pack a bag," he instructed gently. "The *casita's* less than an hour away."

The landscape, which usually engrossed Tori, was more like a brush stroke swirling around her than the soothing, peace-invoking blanket it usually was. Not only was she worried about Barbara's decision, but the tension between her and Jake hadn't lessened since their trip to the toy store. There was so much unsaid between them. Jake's offer to spend the weekend with her had surprised her. Yet, thinking about it now, she knew he was the type of man who would do anything to help anyone.

They stopped at a store for groceries and supplies. As they wound along Route 503, the silence between them built in intensity. By the time they reached Chimayo, purple dusk had surrounded the cliffs, and the reddish-brown earth had dimmed into shadows.

Tori had no idea what to expect as Jake veered off the main road. A short time later he made another turn and she spotted the *casita.* With night enveloping them she couldn't see it very well, but from what she could tell the outside was cream-colored adobe. It was small with a barrel-tiled roof and an attached carport. As they climbed out of Jake's truck, the gravel was loose under her shoes.

Jake led the way, flipping on the light as soon as he opened the door.

The place was utterly charming. The wood-plank floor was old and scarred, but bore a polished patina. A woodstove sat on a Mexican-tiled hearth. Small high windows lent more wall space. A red-and-navy sofa and a comfortable-looking navy armchair angled around the stove, while a lodge-pine table held a wrought-iron lamp with a parchment shade. The kitchen area was tiny, with its two-burner range and small refrigerator. Tori could see into the bedroom, which only had enough room for a double bed, night-stand and highboy chest. There was a handwoven rug, patterned with corn dancers, in front of the sofa. A *kokopelli* hanging was draped on the wall above a small bookcase.

Jake disappeared for a few minutes and returned with Tori's overnight case in one hand, his duffel bag in the other. Although he carried her bag into the bed-room and laid it on the bed, he dropped his duffel behind the sofa.

Did that mean they'd be sleeping separately? If ever Tori needed Jake to hold her, it was tonight.

"I'll get a fire going in the woodstove." He didn't make eye contact.

"I'll put the groceries away."

Jake lit the stove and checked on the supply of fire-wood out back, and Tori started dinner. She put pasta on to boil while she sautéed chicken pieces with on-ions and peppers.

"You didn't have to go to all this trouble," he in-sisted when he returned to the kitchen.

"It kept me busy."

"Busy hands, quiet mind?"

"I wish it worked that way." Putting the lid on the pan, she asked, "Who does this place belong to?"

"Craig Fernandez. I worked with him in Albuquerque until he decided to become a special agent in Chicago with the U.S. Customs Service.''

''He's going to hold on to this place?''

''He inherited it from his uncle. He doesn't want to sell it. I check on it every now and then for him.''

Jake had mentioned Albuquerque, and all the questions she had about the work he used to do came tumbling back. But there was enough tension between them as it was. She didn't want to add to it.

During dinner their conversation was more stilted than it had ever been. After they stowed away the leftovers and cleaned up the dishes, Tori went to the bedroom to use her cell phone. But there were no messages waiting for her on her machine. Unzipping her suitcase, she took out the framed picture of Andy she'd laid on top. When she picked it up, she let all the love she felt for the little boy wash over her.

She didn't even realize she was crying until Jake came into the bedroom. Turning her around to face him, he took her into his arms. ''Shh,'' he whispered into her ear. ''It's going to be all right.''

But she shook her head, feeling as if her world had turned upside down, feeling as if she was losing everything that was important to her, including Jake.

As he held her, both of their hearts started beating faster. In moments, their rhythm seemed to unite, and Tori couldn't tell which was his and which was hers. When Jake's hands moved up and down her back, the long strokes became caresses that soothed and then made her tremble. Cupping her face in his hands, he kissed her tears, then her cheeks, then her mouth.

She'd missed him so.

From the hunger of his kiss, he'd missed her, too.

As he lifted her sweater over her head and tossed it aside, she reached for the buttons on his flannel shirt. Their movements were quick and frenzied...because if either of them thought about this for too long, they'd stop. Each time they came together, Tori fell more in love with Jake. He was nothing like any man she'd ever known. He was strong and good and true.

As he trailed kisses over her breasts, she set to work on his belt buckle. When her fingers unzipped his fly, she heard his sharp intake of breath. He not only had power over her, she had power over him. They gave and they took, partners and equals.

There was raw hunger in Jake tonight. She could feel it in his fingertips, see it in his eyes, read it in his kiss. Everything he did caused trembling and turmoil and pleasure so exquisite she never wanted it to end. His hard arousal told her this foreplay was just for her. But she wanted him to know she didn't need it.

No restraint bound her as her hands explored his chest, then the pulsing male heat. When he backed her up to the bed, they fell onto the mattress. Jake seemed insatiable as his kisses became more intimate, deeper, wetter. His lips and tongue weren't only on hers, but everywhere.

He fingered her nipples, and then laved and suckled them until she cried out, "I need you, Jake!"

"God help me, I need you, too," he murmured, and then trailed kisses lower and lower and lower, until she was grabbing the spread beneath her, squeezing it into her palms. The pleasure he was giving her was so wonderfully, achingly erotic, she couldn't keep still.

His tongue taunted her thighs and then the V between them. She felt as if she'd explode into a million pieces, yet she knew more was coming. His hands slipped under her bottom, lifting her to him. When his tongue probed and then found the bud that had swollen for him, her cry echoed in the room. She'd hardly had a chance to appreciate the wonder of the explosion until he was on his forearms above her, thrusting into her, taking her on another journey with him…into him.

She wrapped her legs around him and took him in deeper. He groaned. When her muscles contracted, he stilled for a few moments. "I want to make this last," he said hoarsely.

She wanted to make it last, too. Because she didn't know what was going to happen next, if they'd ever make love again. Was Jake regretting the tenuousness of their bond? Was he realizing he might want more, too?

All she wanted to do was touch Jake—his body, his heart, his soul. Her hands roamed over his shoulders, then stroked the back of his neck under his thick hair.

He shook his head as he gazed down at her. "I'll lose the battle if you keep doing that."

"But we'll win the war," she murmured.

"Hold on," he said roughly. "We're going to do this together."

She held on—to Jake, to her dreams, to her hope that her life would become everything she imagined it could be. Each of his thrusts was tempered and restrained until she tongued and nipped his earlobe.

"Tori," he protested, as he thrust faster and harder and deeper.

Tori kept her eyes open, watching Jake's every feature. She could lose herself in the passion, but she wanted to see his. She needed to catch the emotion in his eyes and see for herself that she meant more to him than a passing fancy. Jake's brown-black eyes had never been so fascinating. She'd never before seen them filled with such intensity.

His jaw was dark with stubble now, his sensual lips parted as he took in a breath, sank in deeper and said, "Come with me, Tori."

Their rhythm was as old, as primal, as transfixing as the mountains, their pleasure as majestic as the highest peak meeting the bluest sky. She surrendered to the beauty and the awe and the sensations that rippled through her and over her and in her, until Jake cried, "Now," and she was catapulted with him, into that forever place where lovers remember a moment for a lifetime.

She and Jake had made love before—but never like this.

When Jake collapsed on top of her, she loved the weight of him, his breath on her neck, his scent mingling with hers.

After they'd both recovered enough to breathe more normally, Jake shifted onto his side, gazed down at her and stroked a wayward strand of hair from her cheek. She waited, hoping he'd reveal his feelings for her, hoping he'd put into words what she'd seen in his eyes.

When he didn't, she was convinced his walls and defenses were still firmly in place. She had to find out why.

"What happened in Albuquerque, Jake? Please tell me."

He was still for so long that Tori didn't know what to expect. Slowly he intertwined his fingers with hers, then extricated them. "I'm going to get a shot of Craig's bourbon. I'll meet you in the living room. Do you want anything?"

If Jake was going to confide in her, tell her what had turned his life upside down, she wanted to be clearheaded. "No, I'm fine."

After he got out of bed, he stopped to pick up his jeans, then left the room. Tori was afraid that the remoteness would come back into his eyes, that the intimacy they'd shared would be forgotten. But maybe they were about to enter into a different kind of intimacy.

Dressing in the red sweats she'd brought along, she went into the living room and settled on the sofa to wait for him. She heard him moving about the kitchen, apparently putting on a pot of coffee to brew.

But as he came into the living room he carried a glass in his hand with an inch of amber liquid. He'd pulled on his jeans, but the button at the fly was unfastened and he was bare-chested. Tori remembered absolutely everything that had happened in that bed only moments before.

When he sat on the sofa beside her, he left at least a foot of space between them, and she knew he intended that. Plying him with more questions would push him away. She waited patiently.

He took a sip of his drink, then set it on the coffee table. "Marion's mother was right. I got her killed."

Tori clasped his arm. ''I'm sure it wasn't as black-and-white as that.''

''It was as black-and-white as you can get. I was a primary negotiator. I trained men and women under me on the police force. When Marion applied to become a negotiator, I was attracted to her. But I knew if we worked together, nothing could come of it. What we'd get involved in required good rapport, not man-woman tension zipping around, maybe interfering with instincts.''

He leaned back against the sofa cushion. ''Before an officer attends school for negotiations training, we put them through real-time scenarios to see if they have what it takes to do the job. Marion came through it like a pro, and I knew she had the intuition, the sense of timing and the patience to talk down someone who was holding hostages.''

Although Tori was still touching Jake, he seemed to slide away from her emotionally as he went on. ''A negotiations team consists of primary and secondary negotiators, a psychologist, a scribe who documents everything, and other support personnel. Marion had been on call as a secondary negotiator for over six months. Then that day all hell broke loose. A few backup members of the team were down with the flu. When we got the call about the hostage situation at the bank, I was involved in a drug bust. I was informed that a twenty-two-year-old attempted a holdup and he was armed. The bank manager made the mistake of telling him that he'd never get away, that the video cameras would identify him, that he'd pushed the panic button and the police were already alerted.''

Jake stared straight ahead, reliving it. ''I made the decision that Marion should be primary until I got there. From what I understand, she was doing an okay job of it. Time is usually on the negotiator's side. We rarely ever do face-to-face negotiations. But when she was talking to the robber on the phone, she found out there was a child inside. She decided to make a deal with him. If he'd send out the little girl and her mother, Marion would go in.''

When Jake took another sip of his drink, he leaned forward, removing himself from Tori's touch. She didn't know if he was going to continue talking. But then he looked her straight in the eye. ''She wore a vest. She went in against the advice of the psychologist on the team. I was on my way there when the bank robber freaked, and his gun went off. Marion took a bullet in the head, and a bank customer was also killed.''

The woodstove's heat was warming the cabin, but there was a chill around Jake, almost like a force field that kept her at bay. ''Why do you blame yourself?''

''Because I should have let someone else take care of the drug bust. I should have left and handled the bank myself.''

''What choice did you have, Jake?''

He ran his hand over his face. ''I don't know. That's what the P.D.'s psychologist kept asking me. That's what I keep turning around in my head. It shouldn't have gone down like it did. Maybe I was too attracted to Marion to see her flaws. Maybe she wasn't ready to act as primary. Something in my judgment was off, and until I figure out what it was, I can't go back to that work.''

After a momentary pause, she said quietly, ''You can't let your guilt over this ruin your life.''

Standing, he snapped, ''It's *not* ruining my life. I'm moving ahead.''

''Are you?''

''Dammit, Tori. How do you get rid of guilt? It isn't like I can open a window and throw it out. Don't you understand? It's with me all the time. I feel responsible for what happened…responsible for *her.*''

''And now you don't want to be responsible for anyone. But it's in your nature to be a responsible man, to care for others, to help them when they're in trouble, to protect them from danger and heartache. That's why you're so good with Ricky and Ryan, why you checked into Charlie's background, why you're here with me now. There's a war going on inside you, Jake. Until one side wins over the other and you can convince yourself to lay it all to rest, you're not going to know where you want to go or what you want to do.''

Rubbing the back of his neck, he let out a frustrated sigh. ''You're just like the rest, Tori. This isn't as simple as making a decision.''

''I know that. But maybe you need to get back into police work,'' she suggested softly. ''Maybe you need to save other lives.''

''Or *lose* them.''

She could see Jake was still caught in the web of his background, wanting to be a different man than his father was, insisting on freedom, instead of being trapped by a relationship. Marion's death had seemed to drop a cage over him. Somehow he had to find the key to unlock the door.

Tori knew she could help him with more talking, with more touching. Love healed, and the love she felt for him was so strong she knew it could work wonders. But he had to be willing to let it.

"It's probably best if we turn in," he said, ending the conversation. "We can get an early start in the morning, go to White Rock, climb all those steps to the cliff dwellings and hike around. It'll do us both good."

In her opinion, making love with Jake again would do a lot *more* good. But she could see he was bound in memories, trying to remove himself from feelings, not pack on more. She knew making love made him feel—because Jake Galeno was not a callous man. He was a warmhearted, caring man, a man who deserved a wife and a family and a future rich with rewards.

He glanced at his bourbon sitting on the coffee table. Taking it to the sink, he tossed it in. He didn't look at her when he said, "I'll see you in the morning."

He was dismissing her. He was telling her he wanted to be alone, that they wouldn't be sharing the bed or confiding secrets in the middle of the night.

"I'm going to call for messages again and then get a shower," she said. "If you want to talk any more..." She could still hope.

But he shook his head. "I'll probably be asleep before you're out of the shower."

Tori doubted that. She rose from the sofa, longing

to go to him, give him a hug, touch him. But she could see he didn't want that.

"I'll get you up around six."

The pain in Jake's eyes tightened her throat as she left him and went to the bedroom to make her call.

Chapter Thirteen

As the weekend progressed, Tori felt Jake distancing himself from her. It was subtle. He was as solicitous as ever, as protective. But he was careful not to touch her. Their conversations were surface and casual—about the scenery, about the cliff dwellings, about backpacking in the wilderness. They didn't talk about Barbara and Andy, or what had happened in Albuquerque, or what *wasn't* happening between them.

By Saturday evening, they sat in the *casita* together playing chess and listening to a classical-guitar CD they'd found in a small player on the bookshelves. The physical exertion of the day had caught up with Tori and she turned in around ten, while Jake slept on the sofa again. When she awakened at dawn, she found Jake already dressed and a dusting of snow on the ground.

While Tori fixed breakfast, Jake split firewood to replenish the supply they'd used. Afterward, they went for a long hike, mostly in silence. The sun shone brightly on burnished cliffs reaching into white clouds and melting the snow. Tori tried to drink in the azure sky, tried to calm the anxiety in her heart. But each footstep ticked away the minutes until she would know Barbara's decision. Jake seemed lost in his thoughts, too, and she wished she could read his mind.

They started back to Santa Fe after lunch. It didn't take long to pack up everything they'd brought and make sure they'd left the *casita* the way they'd found it.

During the drive home, Jake asked, "What are you going to do if this adoption falls through?"

"I'm not ready to face the possibility of that yet, Jake."

"You can't tell me you haven't been preparing yourself this weekend."

"I've been praying more than preparing, hoping more than despairing. I love Andy."

"Sometimes prayers and love aren't enough."

"I'm not in denial. I do know that. It's just..." Her voice caught and she couldn't find the words to describe what she'd feel if she lost Andy.

For the first time since they'd made love, Jake reached out and covered her hand. "I didn't mean to upset you more, but I'm worried about how you're going to cope if Barbara decides to keep him."

His hand felt so good on hers. Sharing her thoughts with Jake was as natural as breathing. "I've heard about children who are available for adoption in Guatemala. That would be an option. I've also thought about adopting an older child who needs a home. I'm going to be a mother, Jake, one way or another.''

He took his eyes from the road for a couple of seconds to focus on her, and she saw respect there. Seconds later, he released her hand and she keenly felt the loss.

After a short while, Jake pulled up in front of Tori's house and said in a low murmur, ''What have we here?''

Tori had been lost in thought, not looking out the window. Now she gasped as she saw Barbara sitting on her porch steps holding Andy. The baby was dressed in the jacket and hat Tori had bought him with a blanket also wrapped around him. He was crying and Barbara looked upset.

''She wasn't supposed to bring him back until tonight!''

''Maybe she needs your help.''

Tori climbed hurriedly out of Jake's truck and ran to her front porch. ''What's wrong, Barbara? Are you and Andy okay?''

Barbara couldn't seem to wait to shove Andy into Tori's arms. ''I can't do this. It's been a disaster. I can't take care of a baby. I thought they were supposed to sleep all the time. I can't figure out what he wants when he's crying.''

Tori gathered Andy close, and soon his cries became tiny hiccups as she patted his back. ''Barbara, it's not easy. If you'd have called me, I would have come over.''

"Don't you understand? I didn't want you to come over. If I can't do it alone, I can't do it at all."

Tori knew she was digging her own grave, but she had to give this teenager a chance to be a mother. "Everyone needs help."

"*You* don't. Look at him. He wasn't like that for me all weekend. Besides that, I don't *like* taking care of him. I don't *want* to take care of him."

Swaying with the baby, Tori asked, "Then what was this weekend all about?"

Jake had come up beside her now, and he was listening, too.

"I felt I should try and do it. You know, see if it was the right thing? I didn't seem to fit in with my friends anymore, so I thought maybe I should be a mother."

All Tori wanted to do was take Andy inside, hold him to her breast and forget Barbara had ever existed. But she had to do the right thing. She had to do what was best for Andy.

Her heart hurt as she asked, "Do you want to learn *how* to be a mother?"

Barbara's answer was quick, and came with an emphatic shake of her head. "No. I don't know if I'll *ever* want to be a mother—changing diapers, filling bottles, doing laundry. I don't know how women do it. I want to be a doctor and save people's lives, not rock a baby to sleep."

"You have to be sure," Tori insisted. "Once you sign those papers, you're giving up your parental rights for good."

"My lawyer has explained that over and over, and

I know it. After this weekend, I'm sure it's the right thing to do. It's the right thing for Andy." Her eyes held a shimmer of tears now, yet Tori knew that Barbara was putting her son first.

The teenager took a last look at Jake and Tori and the baby. "I have to get home and get the place cleaned up before Mom gets back."

But Tori couldn't just let this girl go, this girl who had given her a gift that was so precious. No thanks would ever be enough. "If you ever want to know how Andy's doing, if you ever want to see him, just call me."

Barbara nodded and then headed for her car. Tori picked up the diaper bag and carried Andy inside.

The scene on the porch had twisted Jake's gut. Both women were putting the baby first. Barbara had a lot of growing up to do. And Tori... He'd just seen her courage and selflessness as she'd dealt with Barbara. They had to have a talk before he left.

A short while later, Andy fell asleep in Tori's arms. Jake could tell how much she'd missed him and simply didn't want to let him go. But as if she understood that was part of mothering, too, she finally laid him back in his crib. Jake waited for her in the living room.

When she entered the room, she seemed to brace herself. She'd obviously sensed Jake had something to say.

"You're an amazing woman."

She stood, facing him, her gaze unwavering. "But?"

"No buts. You're going to be a wonderful mother. Your life will revolve around your son. And you need a man who can give you more than a few nights of great sex.''

''We had more than great sex, Jake. You just don't want to admit it.''

Making love with her on Friday night had unnerved him. He'd never before felt such soul-stirring passion, such deep need, such an overwhelming desire to keep her with him always. But he had a life to settle first.

''We have chemistry, Tori. But you want more than that, and I can't give it.''

Shoving her hands into her jeans pockets, she shook her head. ''I don't think you're the type of man who responds to simply chemistry. You have more to give than any man I know. But I won't try to hold you in a relationship you don't want. I need more than a man who's in and out of my life and Andy's. He needs permanence and stability and a role model who's always around. He needs a man he can count on.''

Each of her words was like a lance in Jake's heart, because he knew she was right. Nevertheless, until he confronted his demons and dumped the guilt, he wasn't right for her. He'd never believed in marriage. But he knew Tori needed the commitment of it in order to give her trust completely. She had to know that a man wouldn't leave her again.

''I think we'd better say goodbye,'' he said.

There were tears in her eyes now, but she didn't argue with him. ''If I happen to run into you, are we just supposed to ignore each other?''

''Of course not,'' he said gently. ''We'll smile and make small talk and go our separate ways. I won't be around that much longer. I've decided to move to Colorado. So in a few weeks, running into me won't be a problem.''

''Then I guess there's nothing else to say.''

He wanted that last kiss, that last look into her eyes that would stay with him for a lifetime. He wanted to run his hands over her skin, tease sighs from her and give her everything she needed. But he couldn't, and that was why he was going to leave.

Leaving Tori standing in her living room with her baby sleeping in the room beyond was the hardest thing he'd ever done.

As Jake stood in Nina's kitchen on Sunday afternoon two weeks later, Charlie sat on the living-room floor helping Ricky adjust the fire engine's ladder to the edge of the sofa. Then he assured Ryan he could dump his load of marbles into the magazine holder.

''They love the presents you gave them.'' Nina set a carton of milk in the refrigerator.

''I'm glad.''

''This afternoon Ricky asked me if Tori was coming to have ice cream and cake with us. I told him I called her, but she was busy today—that's why she sent their presents over yesterday. Was she really busy, Jake? Or was that just an excuse not to be here with you?''

His heart pumped harder at the thought of Tori. ''If she said she was busy today, then she was busy.'' After a short pause he asked, ''Do you know if everything went smoothly with Barbara signing the final papers?''

''You haven't talked to Tori?''

''We've gone our separate ways.''

Nina tapped a helium balloon floating up from one chair with a bit of force. ‘‘You’re so exasperating. If you want to know how the adoption went, call and ask her.’’

‘‘I told you—’’

‘‘I know what you told me. Just like you were wrong about Charlie, you’re wrong about this.’’

Pride made him defend his attitude about Charlie. ‘‘I was concerned you were jumping into a relationship too fast.’’

‘‘And *I’m* concerned you’re never going to jump into a relationship again. You saw Mama’s unhappiness and Dad’s bad temper and blamed it on marriage. But marriage is all about the two people who make the vows. Mama and Dad were wrong for each other. Frank and I were wrong for each other. But Charlie is right for me. And I think Tori is right for you.’’

Jake missed Tori. Her absence in his life was a physical ache that wouldn’t go away. But he’d done the best thing for her. ‘‘Did Barbara sign the final papers?’’ he asked again.

Brushing her hair over her shoulder, Nina studied him. ‘‘Yes, she did. Tori is Andy’s mother. It will be completely official in a few months.’’

He could only imagine Tori’s happiness. The thought that he couldn’t see it gnawed at him.

Needing to plug the hole in his heart, he joined Charlie and the boys and his mother in the living room, remembering something else he’d brought along for Ricky and Ryan. Taking out his wallet, he slipped two silver dollars from the billfold where he’d put them for safekeeping. Now he offered one to each of the boys.

"Wow!" Ricky exclaimed. "It's a big quarter."

Jake laughed. "Not exactly. It's worth the same as a dollar bill." He pulled one of those from his wallet to show them. "It's just more special. That's what I want you to think about. Before you spend it, you have to decide if you want to give up the special silver dollar for something really important, or if you'd rather just keep it."

"What's something really important?" Ryan asked.

"You'll know when you want to give up the silver dollar to get it."

"Neat!" Ricky exclaimed. "I'm gonna put mine in my piggy bank so I don't lose it."

"That's a good idea," Rita Galeno agreed. "Ryan, where are you going to put yours?"

"In our underwear drawer. Nobody'd ever look there. It'll be safe." He ran off to make sure it was.

"I thought giving them the hand-held electronic games would be special for their sixth birthday. But your silver-dollar idea is even better," Charlie said.

"They'll forget the silver dollars and have a ball with the game. You're good for them, Charlie."

The other man studied Jake to see if he was sincere. Seeing that he was, Charlie admitted, "I want to be their dad eventually. Think you can live with that?"

"I think it's exactly what they and Nina need."

Silence filled the room until Charlie said, "They're going to miss you if you leave."

Jake was still holding his wallet. Now, as he started to fold it, the chain from Marion's St. Jude medal slipped out. Tucking it back in, he suddenly realized exactly what he needed to do before he left Santa Fe. "You'll fill the gap."

His mother rose from her chair. "I'm going to make sure those two hooligans aren't getting into mischief." She looked at Jake. "Are you going to stick around to watch the video I gave them?"

"No. There's something I have to do." Slipping Marion's medal out of his wallet, he held it in his palm, closed his fingers around it and followed his mother into the boys' room to say goodbye.

Half an hour later he'd found the address he was looking for. Marion's mother, a widow, lived near the toy store where he and Tori had gone shopping. The tan-colored adobe looked like a box. It was smaller even than Tori's house. The property was well maintained.

There was a car in the gravel driveway. But when Jake knocked on the door, no one answered. Going around back, he found Mrs. Montgomery sweeping off her patio. When she saw him, the broom stilled in her hand and the afternoon shadows seemed to grow longer.

Finally she asked, "What are you doing here?"

"I want to give you something that was Marion's."

Her eyes went wide. "What could you possibly have of hers?"

"We were friends, Mrs. Montgomery. In a different time and a different place, we might have been more. With the nature of the work we were involved in, there couldn't be more." He opened his hand and let the necklace dangle. "Marion told me she bought this and had her priest bless it before she entered the academy. It's St. Jude, the patron saint of desperate causes. She thought she'd need that as a cop.''

''How did you get it? You weren't there when she died.''

''No, I wasn't there. But the week before I had to talk down a jumper from a ledge on Sandia Peak. Marion was there that day, and before I went out on the ledge with him, she gave me this.''

Mrs. Montgomery's eyes filled with tears. ''You must have been very important to her.''

She took another good look at Jake and then propped her broom against the wall of the house. When she returned to the edge of the patio, she took the necklace from him, fingering it gently, letting her tears fall. ''I've been wrong to blame you.''

''No, you haven't been. I sent her in.''

''That was the work she chose, Mr. Galeno. I imagine Marion was chomping at the bit to handle that situation. And pleased that you had enough confidence in her to let her do it.''

''She wasn't ready.''

''She would never have been ready for a man with a gun who pointed it at her and shot. It could have happened next year or five years from now. I've known that all along. When I saw you in that toy store with your basket full of toys, the sadness on your face when I mentioned Marion's name, I knew you were a decent man who cared about my daughter. I knew you didn't put her life in danger callously, with no regard for her. She and I had many arguments about this work she wanted to do. And maybe that was part of it, too.

I felt guilty for not supporting her enough. I suppose we both have to forgive ourselves, don't we.''

Not waiting for his answer, she looked down at Marion's medal in her hand. ''I know my daughter would forgive whatever we thought we did. That was the way she was.''

Jake suddenly felt incredible relief that he had found his way here, incredible relief at hearing Marion's mother's words.

Managing a weak smile, Mrs. Montgomery asked, ''How would you like to come in for a cup of coffee? I can show you pictures of Marion when she was a little girl.''

Jake joined Mrs. Montgomery on the patio. ''I'd like that. I'd like that a lot.''

''We miss Jake, don't we?'' Tori asked Andy as she sat him in his bouncy seat in his crib on Monday morning. She was overjoyed that she was now Andy's mom. But Jake's leaving had pushed her into a sadness she couldn't shake.

''If only he knew how much I love him,'' she said to her son.

Andy's little hands flailed as if in reaction to her words.

''I should have told him. Maybe it would have made a difference.'' But then she remembered the anguish on Jake's face as he'd told her about Marion, as well as his determination when he'd walked out her door. Why did she think a declaration of love would get through to him if nothing else had?

When her phone rang, she switched on the music

box on Andy's mobile and hurried to the bedroom to get it. She carried the cordless phone back into the baby's room.

"Tori, it's Loretta. I've picked up some kind of flu bug and I can't go in today. I'm so sorry. I tried to call Mary Beth, but no one's answering."

Tori had intended to stay home today, then spend the afternoon and evening tomorrow at the gallery for Renée's show. All the details were finalized. Everything was ready. Mary Beth wasn't scheduled to work today, and Loretta had told her she'd take care of the whole day. Now it looked as if plans were going to change.

"That's okay. I've already given Andy his bath and fed him. I just have to get dressed. I'll be able to open the gallery on time."

"Are you sure you can handle it alone with Andy?"

"If I can't—and I can't reach Mary Beth—I'll close for the rest of the day."

"But if you lose sales—"

"When did you turn into a worrywart? Andy's going to be as good as gold. I'll be able to put in a full day and even package up some of those Internet orders. I'll be fine, Loretta. Really."

"I'll be there tomorrow morning, no matter what."

"No, you're going to take care of yourself. I'm sure I can get hold of Mary Beth sometime today. Maybe next week we can interview for more part-time help."

After Tori switched off the phone, she gathered Andy up, bouncy seat and all. Working today would do her good. Maybe at the gallery tears wouldn't be so close to the surface. Maybe at the gallery she could forget that Jake was no longer in her life.

As Jake drove home from the lumberyard, he was still remembering his visit with Marion's mother last night. He felt as if a great weight had been lifted from his shoulders. Maybe he should have explained everything to her sooner. On the other hand, neither of them might have been ready sooner to confront Marion's death.

The supplies he'd picked up rattled in the back of his truck as he drove up Old Santa Fe Trail. He'd intended to simply drive by the plaza where Tori's shop was located. He'd done that many times in the past week—maybe to prove to himself the emptiness in his chest would diminish each successive time. But it hadn't, and he found himself turning in there now. After all, he had to return her key. If Loretta was there, he'd find out how Tori and Andy were doing. If Tori was there...he'd see her one last time. She probably wouldn't be there. The middle of the afternoon would be Andy's nap time.

Yet as Jake parked in front of the string of stores, the Open sign beckoned him. Two women carrying wrapped packages stepped outside. He held the door, then stepped over the threshold. Immediately he saw Andy's crib a few feet from the cashier's desk. Tori was repositioning a painting on the west wall.

She glanced over her shoulder when she heard the bell, and her eyes widened. "Jake!"

The sight of her made his breath catch and he realized this had been a mistake. Taking the key ring from his pocket, he said, "I wanted to return this."

Her expression went blank, and then she squared her shoulders. "I see."

"I'll be leaving at the end of next week."

They were so engrossed in each other, neither of them turned when the security bell rang. But seconds later, Jake's instincts went on alert when he heard the click of the door being locked from inside.

As he turned, he saw a blond, burly man of about six-four, who matched the sketch Phil had shown him, holding a 9-mm semiautomatic trained on Tori and then him.

"This place has been too damned busy today," the armed man muttered. "It was now or never."

Fear stole over Tori's face as she reflexively stepped closer to her son's crib.

"Stay put!" the gunman yelled.

Assessing the situation in an instant, Jake's training told him not to play hero. If he could manage to hit Tori's silent alarm, dispatch would call to find out if it was a false alarm or the real thing.

Keeping his body stance nonaggressive, his voice calm, he offered, "My wife's worried about our son. He's been fussy for a few days. She's afraid he might be getting sick."

The armed man kept his gaze on Jake, but moved toward the crib. "He looks okay to me."

In the moment the man's attention was diverted, Jake slipped his hand into his jacket pocket, felt for the right buttons and pressed the speed-dial for Phil's desk number. If he was there, maybe Jake could make himself heard.

''He just fell asleep,'' Tori offered in a shaky voice, seeing what Jake was doing.

Adrenaline rushed through Jake and he controlled it as he'd learned to do. Slow and easy was best. He didn't want to alert the gunman or do anything to put Andy and Tori in more jeopardy than they were already in. If anything happened to either of them…

Nina's words rang in his ears. *Mama and Dad were wrong for each other. Frank and I were wrong for each other. But Charlie is right for me and I think Tori is right for you.*

In a lightning-quick moment of awareness, Jake felt his love for Tori with every fiber of his being. The attraction and the bond they'd always shared *was* more than chemistry. How had he ever imagined he could walk away from her? How could he have ever imagined a life without her?

He'd used nobility to cover his despair. He'd told himself that walking away was the best thing for her. If he walked away, he'd never hurt her. If he walked away, he'd never feel trapped. He suddenly and completely realized that loving Tori and Andy would free him!

Now he just had to get them all out of this so he could tell her.

Moving slowly toward the cashier's desk and the silent alarm, he tried to think and react beyond his newfound love for Tori. When she looked at him with beseeching eyes, he knew he'd die for her. He just hoped he didn't have to.

Chapter Fourteen

"Don't move!" the gunman commanded, looking panicked.

His yell startled Andy, who began to cry.

"Sorry," Jake said. "I'm just worried about the baby. Maybe you could let my wife hold him."

If Tori walked around the crib, she could step on the alarm. The gunman wouldn't know exactly where it was located—or that it was on the floor.

As Andy cried, Tori's gaze met Jake's. She understood. He could tell.

When Andy's cries became louder, the gunman gave in. "Okay. Pick him up. Just don't go anywhere near that cash register."

Nodding, Tori started toward the crib, rounding the front.

As casually as he could, Jake asked, ''What do you want, Mr....'' He purposefully let his words trail off.

The burly man's eyes swung to Jake's. ''You don't gotta know my name. I want as many of these paintings and statues as I can stow in my van. *You* can help load them. I knew the day before a show by Ludwig this place would be full of stuff.'' He glanced at his watch. ''I gotta meet my fence in an hour.''

Jake hadn't seen a van. The robber must have parked it out back. Out of the corner of his eye, Jake noticed Tori's foot swing toward the desk, and then she lifted Andy from the crib.

''Why artwork?'' He wanted to engage this guy in dialogue and find some common ground.

''Easy to fence them. There's plenty of private collectors who don't want to pay gallery prices.''

Jake nodded his understanding. As Andy quieted in Tori's arms, he said, ''I hear some of those collectors sit in a room with their paintings and don't show them to anyone. Seems like a waste. Don't you think so?''

''I don't care what they do with the stuff as long as I get my cut.''

''Why don't you tell me your first name?'' Jake suggested. ''It will make it easier to talk. My name's Jake. This is my wife, Tori.'' If he could convince this guy to see them as people with relationships and connection, he might not be as quick to hurt them.

''We ain't gonna talk. You're gonna load my van, and I'm gonna get the hell out of here.''

When the phone rang, the gunman pointed his weapon at Tori and Andy. ''Don't touch it,'' he growled.

But Jake countered, ''If she doesn't answer, it might keep ringing.''

''I'm expecting a call,'' Tori added. ''A customer is supposed to call and check if I have his purchases packaged and ready for pickup. I can tell him they won't be ready until tomorrow.''

''You don't want another customer trying to get in while you're loading the artwork,'' Jake said matter-of-factly.

''What do you care?'' the man asked with a wave of his gun.

''I don't want anyone to get hurt,'' Jake said sincerely. If he could just stall this guy... Trying to disarm him could put Tori and Andy in harm's way.

The phone kept ringing.

''All right. Answer the damn thing,'' the man said to Tori.

Jake was proud of Tori as she answered and pretended to know the caller. He could tell by her one-word answers that she was responding to the dispatcher's questions.

She ended with, ''I'll definitely have those paintings ready tomorrow.'' Then she hung up the phone.

''Good job,'' the thief said. ''Now let's get things moving.'' His gaze swerved back and forth between the two of them. ''The problem is it's gonna be hard keeping my eye on both of you. So...''

He walked over to Tori and snarled, ''Give him to me.''

Every nerve in Jake's body, every emotion in his head, was screaming. He could only imagine what

Tori was feeling. When the man pointed the gun at Andy, she had no choice.

"Please don't hurt him," she whispered as she let the gunman take Andy.

"Oh, I'm not gonna hurt him. Not unless one of you does something you shouldn't."

Andy began squirming and crying again. The anguish on Tori's face tore at Jake's gut.

"Look," Jake said, getting the man's attention again. "Let my wife hold our son. I can carry anything you want out to the van."

Andy's squalls grew in intensity and the man looked jittery.

"All right. But I've got her and your kid in my sights. You make one wrong move—"

"I won't make a wrong move," Jake assured him calmly. "You tell me exactly what you want me to do, and I'll do it."

Stalling as much as he could, Jake carried the paintings to the van in the back, all the while keeping his attention on the man, the gun and Tori. He knew if a SWAT team arrived, they'd try to do it silently.

Unfortunately the odds were good the armed robber wouldn't let them go—he and Tori could identify him.

Jake had just carried the last canvas to the van when the phone rang again. This time the robber said, "You ain't answering. Forget it." He waited and after twenty rings, the instrument stopped.

That had to be the negotiator, Jake thought, wondering if Phil Trujillo could hear anything from the cell phone.

Suddenly a loud male voice boomed into the gallery

from a public-address system outside. ''You're surrounded. Come out the front door with your hands on top of your head.''

Jake could see that the armed man was truly panicky now, which was the last thing he wanted. In an even tone he suggested, ''Let me open the door and show them that we're all right. If I do, they'll give you time to think about this.''

The burly man's eyes darted here and there—at Tori, at Jake, at the storage room.

''They're going to have the SWAT team in position,'' Jake offered in a conversational tone. ''If you make the wrong move, you're going to get killed.''

''Why do you care?''

''Because if you get shot, one of us might get hurt, too. I want my wife and son safe.'' He'd never meant or felt anything more.

''I wanna get out of here. I just wanna drive away with the loot.''

''All right. Are those your terms for letting us go?''

Without answering Jake, the gunman peered out the window again. Then he nodded. ''I just wanna drive away.''

Jake ran through various scenarios in his head. He needed to make contact with whoever was leading the team outside.

The man suddenly erupted. ''I can't let you all go! If I do that, they'll shoot out my tires and take me down a block from here. Someone has to go with me. Maybe the woman and the kid. They wouldn't dare shoot with them in the van.''

Jake's heart dropped to the pit of his stomach. ''You

don't want a baby with you. He'll be crying and screaming and need to be fed and changed. He'll give you away if you do try to hide somewhere.''

''Then I'll take the woman. She won't give me any fits.'' He motioned to Tori. ''Give your hubby the baby.''

The expression on Tori's face said that she'd do anything to save her son, and him, even though she was scared to death. As she started toward him, Jake gave a minuscule shake of his head, telling her he didn't want to take Andy. He wouldn't be free to move if he had to.

The phone rang again. This time their captor took aim at it and fired, then fired again. Turning to the window, he shot through it. As he swung around toward Tori, instincts prevailed and Jake moved. He knew if he didn't, he'd lose the woman he loved.

''Down!'' he shouted to Tori.

He rushed the gunman, his leg going up and kicking the gun out of the man's hand. As the weapon skimmed across the floor, Jake got him in a choke hold and forced him to the door. As soon as he pushed the man over the threshold, the police were on him, shouting for him to get down on the ground.

When Jake let go, someone else took over.

Jake watched as officers pushed the man to the ground and handcuffed him. Sure the thief wouldn't be causing any more trouble, Jake strode back into the gallery and found Tori sitting on the floor against the counter with Andy cradled in her arms.

At first he thought she might have been injured.

Fear gripping him, he crouched down to her and asked, ''Are you hurt?''

As Tori looked into Jake's eyes, she shook all over. When he'd pushed the gunman out of the gallery, she'd found all her strength had left her. At his shout, she'd gone down into a crouch and then stayed on her knees. After she realized they were all safe, she'd felt light-headed and decided it was better to stay on the floor.

She'd loved Jake before today, before he'd saved their lives. Now she realized how absolutely essential he was to her life—and Andy's. She had to tell him she loved him. She had to convince him that together they could face anything.

''I'm fine,'' she managed at his concerned look.

To prove it, she started to get up.

But she had help. Jake reached for her and pulled her and Andy up into his arms. When he buried his face in her neck, she could feel his deep, lung-filling breath as he seemed to realize they were both safe, too.

Then he raised his head and gazed into her eyes. ''I love you, Tori Phillips. I want to spend the rest of my life with you—if you'll let me. I've been an idiot thinking I could walk out of your life and Andy's. I can't. And I won't.''

She couldn't believe what Jake was saying to her. ''Are you sure? Maybe this isn't the best time—''

He took her face between his big hands. ''You don't get it, Tori. This *is* the best time. Now I know exactly what you and Andy mean to me.''

''I don't want you to feel trapped. I don't want you to regret—''

''My only regret is that I've waited this long to come to my senses. I saw Marion's mom. We had a long talk. She doesn't blame me anymore, and I think I've stopped blaming myself, too. Marion made a decision that day that kept a mother and child safe. When that man started shooting, I had to make a decision, too. I want a life with you. I want a family. I want to stop running from the past and look forward to the future. Will you marry me?''

She could see in his eyes that he'd meant everything he'd said. He was ready for love. Ready for *her* love.

''Yes, I'll marry you!'' she answered joyfully.

His lips sought hers and he kissed her then with the fervor and hunger and need of a man who knows exactly what he wants.

After a few moments, Andy began squirming in Tori's arms, and Jake broke away, smiling. ''I know, little guy. You deserve my attention, too. You're going to get plenty of it.'' Taking Andy from Tori's arms, he put the baby to his shoulder. When he brought Tori close again, he held on to her, just relishing the feel of her in his arms.

Phil Trujillo came into the gallery. ''I've got to get your statements,'' he said with a serious expression.

Jake patted Andy's back. ''No problem.''

''Before I do that, though, the chief said to tell you you've got a job whenever you want one.''

When Tori looked up at Jake, she could see he was considering it.

''Tell the chief I'll come in sometime this week and

talk to him about it.'' He grinned at Phil. ''But before I consider resuming a career, I'm going to get married.''

When he kissed Tori's temple, she realized that the man she loved was finally at peace. They would weave their dreams together and stand side by side no matter what the future might bring.

Epilogue

Red, blue and yellow balloons floated in the corners of Nina's kitchen. A computer-generated banner with the words, HAPPY ADOPTION streamed down the center of the dining-room table. Andy was fourteen months old, and Tori had officially been his mother for eight months. Now Jake was officially his dad.

Jake handed Tori the cake knife as they stood on either side of Andy in his high chair. "Do you want to do the honors?" he asked.

Charlie Nexley chimed in from where he was sitting, "Now that you're officially a father, maybe I'll become one, too."

Charlie and Nina had been married a month ago. They were still in their honeymoon stage—the same stage Jake hoped he and Tori would be in for the rest of their lives.

Nina playfully jabbed her husband's arm. "You're already a dad."

"I mean officially. I'd like to adopt Ricky and Ryan."

The tears Jake saw come to his sister's eyes told him better than any words that she and Charlie were right for each other and that she couldn't want anything more.

Jake felt the same way with Tori.

He knew now that Nina had been right. Tori was indeed the right person for him. Marriage had come to mean a freeing, life-giving chance to explore the world with someone else. Each and every day Tori and Andy enriched his world, and he didn't even want to imagine life without them. He was working for the Santa Fe Police Department now, teaching negotiations skills. He was also on call when special situations arose. He'd been doing the lecture circuit, too, at colleges and law-enforcement conferences. Whenever possible, Tori and Andy went with him. Tori had more help at the gallery, and life couldn't be any more perfect.

Except…

When Andy stuffed cake and icing into his mouth with his fingers, Jake laughed, along with Tori, Nina and Charlie, Ricky and Ryan, and his mom. The icing was smeared all over Andy's fingers, on the tip of his nose and in his hair. But Tori just looked on with that tender sparkle in her eyes she always had for their son.

A short time later, the twins grabbed their jackets and ran into the yard to play with Charlie. Nina and Rita had gone into the living room.

Jake kissed icing from Andy's nose, then kissed his wife. Passion rose, hot and hungry. That was always the way it was between them.

Tori laughed as he broke away. "You taste good," she said.

''So do you.''

''Uh-oh. That look in your eye says Andy's bath is going to be a short one tonight.'' Her smile was wide.

''Is that okay with you, Mrs. Galeno?''

''You know it's always okay with me, Mr. Galeno.''

This was as good a time as any to bring up a subject that had been on his mind. ''With Sean and your mom moving out to Albuquerque in a couple of months, we're going to have plenty of baby-sitters.''

''I love the idea of them retiring out here. Are you afraid Andy's going to get too spoiled?''

''Just to make sure he doesn't, I was wondering what you thought about adopting another baby.''

''Really? I've been thinking about it, but…''

His arm went around her. ''But what?'' They didn't keep secrets from each other.

''But I want our honeymoon to last.''

''Whether we adopt another baby or not, our honeymoon is going to last as long as we're married. Maybe even longer.''

Her expression was radiant as she responded, ''Then I'd love becoming a mother again.''

Jake's kiss this time was a fervent commitment to their vows. He would love, honor and cherish Tori Phillips until the end of time.

* * * * *

Watch for Karen Rose Smith's next
Silhouette Special Edition,
TAKE A CHANCE ON ME,
coming in March 2004.

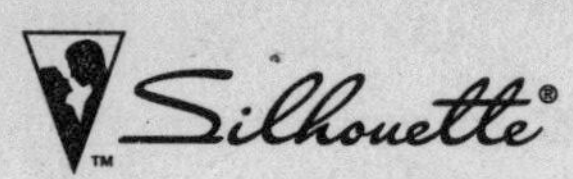

SPECIAL EDITION®

COMING NEXT MONTH

#1591 SECRETLY MARRIED—Allison Leigh
Turnabout
Cool and composed, Delaney Townsend arrived on Turnabout Island only to discover that she was still married to her supposedly ex-husband, Samson Vega. Reuniting with the handsome and brooding sheriff stirred emotions and desires that Delaney had believed long forgotten. Could theirs be a love to last a lifetime?

#1592 COUNTDOWN TO BABY—Gina Wilkins
Merlyn County Midwives
Cecilia Mendoza yearned for motherhood, not the complications of having a husband. So she convinced overworked corporate executive Geoff Bingham to father her child—with no strings attached. But their lighthearted affair quickly turned to something more…something that felt dangerously like love!

#1593 THE VIRGIN'S MAKEOVER—Judy Duarte
Logan's Legacy
Living in the shadow of her outgoing sister was second nature to Lissa Cartwright…until she met Sullivan Grayson. She'd hired the flirtatious entrepreneur to help her with her family's struggling vineyard, never expecting to be the object of his desires. Would Lissa's awakening passion reveal the beauty within?

#1594 LOVE ON CALL—Shirley Hailstock
Working in the E.R. was hectic enough. First-year resident Mallory Russell didn't need the unwelcome attraction to enigmatic pediatric surgeon Bradley Clayton to further confuse her. But the two doctors were drawn together like moths to a flame…and in each other's arms found something that neither could walk away from.

#1595 DOWN FROM THE MOUNTAIN—Barbara Gale
When the terms of a will forced David Hartwell and Ellen Candler together, the sweet and sheltered Ellen, blind since her youth, had a special quality that brought out the tenderest feelings in David. But he feared that once she underwent the surgery that would restore her sight, she would see all of his secrets…and deem him unworthy of her love.

#1596 FORTUNE FINDS FLORIST—Arlene James
The Richest Gals in Texas
Inheriting a fortune had been the easy part for instant millionaire Sierra Carlson. Now what to do with the money? Local farmer Sam Jayce came up with the perfect business plan—one that meshed her career dreams with his. But working closely with Sam and all his warmth and charm inspired dreams of a different sort!

SSECNM0104